Other Books by Greg Smrdel:

Hurricane Izzy - An OBX Story
Home Sweet Outer Banks Home?
The Andy Griffith Show Complete Trivia Guides, Vol. I & II
Trivia Night: Answers You Wished You Knew - 3 Volumes

www.amazon.com/author/gregsmrdel

www.gregsmrdel.com

Published by Milepost 11 Publishing - 2018

Author's Note:

This is a story of a man looking for his family's identity. His mother and father are both gone and Edward Drummond Thatcher Junior, the main character, realizes life has gotten in the way of knowing his family's history. The story takes Edward to some extraordinary places where he meets some extraordinary people, all while in search of answers to his questions.

My love of the Outer Banks continues in this novel. Part of the setting takes place at a fictional magazine office and a house in Nags Head. The other part of the story takes place in Bath, North Carolina, the former home of the notorious Blackbeard the pirate.

Fans of the Outer Banks will recognize the places in the story. Likewise, those in Bath.

Many thanks go out to several people for their support and encouragement, most notably to my wife Char Smrdel. Without her love and wisdom, my books would never see the light of day.

Thanks to Natasha Dankovich for the cover design. The story could be great, but unless there is a provocative cover, most people would never discover it. Sadly, people do judge a book by its cover, and Natasha is the best at making my books stand out.

Also, a huge thank you to those that have read my books and continue to encourage me to write others. Your kind words inspire me to keep going.

Greg Smrdel

Chapter 1 - Ocracoke Inlet

We don't know what the weather was like on November 22, 1718 on Ocracoke Island, North Carolina. That was the date Lieutenant Robert Maynard brought the two sloops he commanded into the channel at daybreak. The weather service doesn't have records going back that far. In fact, much of what we do know about that day's events, in that place, are sketchy at best. What historians have been able to put together is that at some time just past daybreak, Lieutenant Maynard aboard and in command of the "Jane," with Mister Hyde aboard the "Ranger," were spotted by the "Adventure" and were fired upon almost immediately. The broadside causing Maynard to lose almost a third of his men in a single instant.

What needs to be known is that The "Adventure" was no ordinary sailing ship. It was a pirate ship. And it was commanded by one of the fiercest cutthroats of all time, Blackbeard the Pirate.

Once Blackbeard fired the opening volley, he cut the anchor cable on his ship and set sail directly at both the "Jane" and the "Ranger." A battle ensued utilizing both cannons and small arms. However, Lieutenant Maynard still had a cunning trick up his sleeve. He kept many of his men below deck in anticipation of being boarded by the blood-thirsty pirate and his crew. Maynard's trickery worked. Blackbeard, thinking the boat was nearly defenseless threw his grappling hooks over to the "Jane" and pulled her close. The pirate crew then threw several grenades made from powder and shot-filled bottles across the enemy deck. Once the smoke cleared they boarded the "Jane," happy to see only a small contingency of men at the ship's stern. But much to the Pirate leader and crew's surprise, the rest of Maynard's men suddenly busted out of the holds below, shouting and firing at the mangy group of pirates. Maynard's surprise worked as the cutthroats were totally caught off guard.

Blackbeard himself, following a long hand-to-hand battle with Robert Maynard, was ultimately killed by a group of Maynard's men. It was determined that the fearless pirate had been shot five times and cut twenty by sword and cutlass. The pirate's headless body was unceremoniously thrown into the inlet where it is said, "it swam around the sloop three times, before disappearing beneath the bloody waters." His head, then mounted on the bowsprit of Maynard's ship as warning to other pirates as to what their fates may become.

Chapter 2 - Modern Day - Bath, North Carolina

The attic was hot. Stifling hot. The heat and humidity made it so that he couldn't stay in there for all that long. It was not like yesterday; cold, rainy and blustery. The perfect weather day for a funeral. And that's where he was, his father's funeral. But today, Edward Drummond Thatcher Jr. finds himself in his father's attic going through years and years of clutter.

Edward grew up in Bath, living on King Street, until he went away to school in Chapel Hill. He got his degree in journalism, worked as a reporter for several tv stations in the Virginia Beach market and now lives on the Outer Banks of North Carolina, in Nags Head, operating a small magazine.

Bath is an old town. In fact, North Carolina's oldest. The town has been in existence since 1705 as a port on the Pamlico River. It was North Carolina's capital city for a short time in the early 1700s, at a time when one of her more (in)famous citizens was none other than Blackbeard the Pirate.

Blackbeard had settled in Bath around 1718 and took Mary Ormond as his wife after receiving the "royal pardon" offered by the Crown of England. The pardon allowed the pirate captain to be forgiven of all past sins and to become a respectable citizen.

Not much has changed about Bath in the present day. The town lies entirely within the original boundaries as laid out by John Lawson, her founding father. The access to her waters for activities like water skiing, kayaking and wake-boarding has made the town a destination for tourists to congregate during the summer vacation months.

From the time he was a little boy, attending Bath Elementary just down the street about a tenth of a mile, Edward's dad, had always said that he'd pass on the family history to him one day. Sadly, that day never came, and now it was too late. Following a very quick bout with pancreatic cancer, Edward Senior was gone. Father and son Thatcher, living out the real life version of Harry Chapin's "Cat's in the Cradle."

"I've long since retired, my son's moved away
I called him up just the other day
I said "I'd like to see you if you don't mind"
He said "I'd love to, dad, if I can find the time..."

In the stifling heat of the attic, wiping the sweat from his face with the University of North Carolina t-shirt he was wearing, Edward thought to himself that life had gotten too much in the way. He then made a vow that if he couldn't hear the family history from his father, well, then he'd find it out for himself. And he would start here in this collection of "clutter." Unfortunately due to the heat, it just wouldn't be today.

Edward's mother Pam had died a few years before from breast cancer. As an only child it was up to him to clean out the family home. What he ultimately would do with it, he wasn't quite sure yet.

Worn down by the heat, Edward climbed down from the attic, but not before he grabbed a dusty book out of one of his dad's steamer trunks. Trying to take in the gentle breeze off the river, Edward went outside to the screened in porch with a sweet tea and opened the book. The book appeared to be ancient. The title not even readable any longer on the front cover. Edward opened it very carefully and looked at the first page. In smudged black ink he was able to make out its title "*Pyrates and Buccaneers of the Carolinas*."

As Edward leafed carefully through the brittle pages he saw names and stories of people like Calico Jack, along with Mary Read & Anne Bonney (the female pirates), Stede Bonnet and of course the most famous of all, Blackbeard.

Even though Edward and Blackbeard lived in the same town in different places in time, Edward never paid much attention to the history and lore surrounding the pirate. It seemed Edward's only reference to Blackbeard was the pizza, ice cream and putt-putt course a few blocks away. Not a particularly fitting image for a blood-thirsty cutthroat, Edward thought. Edward would sometimes wonder what Blackbeard may have thought looking up from hell with the devil at his side, as a family plays a quick round of mini golf and then reward themselves with ice cream cones beneath his twenty-foot likeness. Complete with smoke, recreating the smoldering tapers the pirate would tuck into his beard. "Certainly not the legacy the pirate captain would have thought he would have left," Edward chuckled to himself.

Edward continued leafing through the well worn pages of the book until the feeling of hunger began to hit. Edward looked at his watch, it was closing in on 4 in the afternoon. It was then that he remembered that he hadn't had lunch yet. So Edward lifted his achy, tired and sweaty body from the rickety old rocking chair and went back in the house to take a shower. Once cleaned up and dried off, Edward slipped on a pair of beige cargo shorts, a fresh Coastal Edge Surf Shop t-shirt and flip flops, and went down the road to the Old Country Kitchen on Carteret Street for an early dinner. Less than a half-mile from the house, it was a place his father would often come in the years after Edward's mother died. "No one else in the house to eat", Edward Sr. used to say, "no need to make a fuss in the kitchen just for me."

Edward Jr. was seated near the front window by the hostess. She said her name was Katie and she would be bringing him his water, and that Natalie would be by to take his order. It wasn't more than three minutes before a young girl came to the table.

"Hi! I'm Natalie, and I'll be your server today." She was dressed in khakis, a Old Country Kitchen green golf shirt and an Old Kitchen baseball cap. Natalie took Edward's order of sweet tea and the fried chicken with mashed potatoes special. As he waited for his drink to arrive, Edward got up from his chair to take a look at all the photos on the wall. It had been what seemed like forever since he was last here. Apparently, his dad was quite the regular, more than Edward had even realized, since he was in nearly half the photos.

One of the pictures caught Edward's attention almost immediately. Edward figured it was a Halloween party since everyone in the picture was dressed in costume. It was his dad, dressed as Blackbeard. The resemblance was uncanny. At least in the pictures that Edward had seen of Blackbeard throughout the years. As he studied it closely, up from behind a kindly voice said "your paw, he was the best Blackbeard we ever had in 'dis here town. So sorry to hear of his passing."

Edward, startled by the voice, turned quickly to find himself standing eye to eye with what can only be describing as on "old salt." The man, skin like leather, as if he had been at sea most of his life, said his name was Petey. Petey continued, "Yep. When we needed someone to play the old pirate captain, there ain't no one better at it than yer paw."

"You knew my dad?" Edward asked.

"Knew him. Knew yer maw too." Petey said as he thrust his hand forward.

Edward accepted it as the old salt introduced himself as Captain Pete Dussault. "But most folks 'round town, they just call me Capt'n Petey."

"Nice to know you Capt'n Petey. Missed you at the funeral yesterday."

"You mighta missed me, my boy, but I didn't miss it. Your paw and me, we said our goodbyes a few days 'afore he died. I'm not good on the ceremony of death. I told him what I had to say and he told me what he had to say and that, I expect, was all that needed to be done."

Natalie came back to the table carrying a plate with enough fried chicken and mashed potatoes to feed an army. Edward asked Captain Petey to join him and the old sea captain readily agreed.

Looking up to the young server, Captain Petey said he'd have his regular, but Edward interjected. "No capt'n, please, have half of this. There's no way I can eat all of this. Natalie, please just bring us another set of silverware and a clean plate."

"And a Budweiser too, if you don't mind Natalie." Looking to Edward with a twinkle in his eye, the captain said, "Got to wash the vittles down me laddie."

The old sea captain and the now fatherless young man had a nice dinner together. Capt'n Petey telling Edward that his father took it hard, real hard when Pam died. "He was like a man that had no purpose in life anymore. Then your paw, he began playing the pirate captain for the town and county fairs around here, and fer the schools too. Kindly gave him a reason to go on. Least ways, that's how I seen it."

Edward, knowing that he had been away for a good long time and really hadn't checked in on his widowed father enough, suddenly felt very guilty. "I'm glad he had you around Capt'n Petey. Doesn't appear I was too much a good son."

"Boy, yer paw, all he ever did was talk about you. He was so proud of his boy that has his own magazine empire up there on the Outer Banks."

Chuckling softly Edward said, "Well, one magazine doesn't an empire make." Wanting to know more, Edward asked, "So what was it he had to say to you?"

"How's that boy?"

"You said that you had to say to my dad what you had to say before he died and he said to you what he had to say. What did he say?"

Capt'n Petey looked off toward the ceiling, rubbing the scruff of a white beard that was on his chin before he spoke. And when he did speak, his eyes locked right onto Edward's eyes. Eyes, green as the sea and were as piercing as Edward ever before experienced. "Boy, I've been studyin' about that. I don't think you can know that right now."

For obvious reasons Edward was confused as to why the captain would say something like that. The look on his face apparently giving away his confusion.

"Look boy," Capt'n Petey said. "You gonna be around these parts awhile?"

"I figure to," Edward responded. "I need to clean out my father's house and decide what to do with it. Plus I promised myself I'd do something while I'm here. Something my dad and I had been promising each other for a good long time now. But, unfortunately time had run out on us, and now, well, I'll just have to figure some things out on my own."

"I'm glad to hear you say that sonny. But if what your talkin' about is what I think you're talkin' about, you may not have to figure it out all by your lonesome. Thanks for dinner me boy. That fried chicken is what this ol' sea captain needed."

With that Capt'n Petey rose from the table and started for the door. The bell perched on top ringing as he opened it. With Edward watching through the window from his table, Captain Petey disappeared into the late afternoon sun.

Chapter 3

That night Edward slept in his old bedroom. His mother and father hadn't changed a thing since Edward moved out before going to college. The walls still decorated with the ribbons and certificates of his teenage achievements. Among a fistful of second and third place ribbons colored in yellow and green, hung the blue first place ribbon in the 200 yard individual medley for the school's swim team. The highest batting average certificate from his senior year at Washington High School, in neighboring Washington, North Carolina, was slightly askew as it hung in the imitation wood grained frame. Washington, North Carolina was commonly referred to as "Little Washington" to distinguish it from the much larger Washington D.C. Little Washington is located on the northern bank of the Pamlico River, and Edward was a star "Pam Packer" back in the day.

As it often did, "Pam Pack" made Edward giggle each time he thought of it. The school adopted the name for their athletic teams to honor the Pamlico Meat Packing plant that sponsored the schools first football team. The nickname, Edward thought, just didn't seem to strike fear into the hearts of their opponents.

Edward laid there a good long while that night, not sleeping. The oppressive heat from the day had suddenly struck up some rather large thunderstorms in the area. He listened to the loud rumbles of thunder as they reverberated off the surrounding houses and buildings in town. First quietly, then with time, louder than before, as the storm crept closer and closer to Bath, North Carolina. Suddenly bright bolts of lightening lit up the dark bedroom. But this wasn't like ordinary lightening. With lightening, usually there's a flash and then darkness before the next bolt would re-illuminate the room. This was a light that lit and stayed lit.

Edward clambered out of his bed and peered through the upstairs window from his family home on King Street and looked southward. The light was continuous. It didn't come on and go away like lightening would. Even though it was raining at a pretty good clip and the winds were picking up, Edward was curious. He ran downstairs and threw a raincoat over his shorts and t-shirt, and with bare feet he went outside to investigate. Not being able to see much past his own street, Edward rushed the half-mile down Carteret to South Main Street to Bonner's Point. Still barefoot, Edward climbed up on one of the benches that lined the park and looked south down Bath Creek.

Growing up in Bath, Edward of course had always heard about "Teach's Light," but he never actually experienced it for himself. Legend says that on nights of violent storms, a light, larger than the size of a man's head, can be seen sailing back and forth from Blackbeard's old homestead on Plum Point across the Bath Creek to Archbell Point to the west. The best way that Edward could explain it, was seeing a ball of fire drifting back and forth, from one point of land to the other. It wasn't being carried away by the winds or the rain, but rather it kept on a consistent path. Until suddenly........It was gone. Poof! Just like that, it had disappeared.

Edward, now completely soaked from the pounding rain and the wind driving water underneath his raincoat, sat on the park bench for several more minutes. He sat there and wondered if what he saw was really Teach's Light. What else could it be, he thought? Not one to believe in legends and unsubstantiated claims, Edward now found himself doubting his own belief system. Slowly Edward began the short walk back to his family home. He thought it strange he was the only one outside investigating the light. Surely he couldn't have been the only one to have seen it.....Could he?

Back home, Edward pulled off the wet clothes. He dried off using a clean towel from the laundry room and changed into a dry pair of sweats and a t-shirt. He picked up his cell phone about to call the Bath Police concerning the strange occurrence he had just witnessed, but a quick glance at the wall clock in the kitchen told Edward that it was 2 am. Calling them now may take the remainder of what little of the night was left. No, better try to get some sleep and place that call in the morning.

Edward climbed the stairs back up to his childhood bedroom. He laid back down on his childhood bed and tried to once again fall asleep.

Chapter 4

The next morning sunlight came blazing into Edward's bedroom window. The sun was out with a vengeance, already threatening to equal the oppressive heat from the previous day. Edward swung his legs off the bed and stood up slowly. He was shocked at how sore he had become from working up in the attic. He did keep himself in fairly decent shape by swimming a couple of miles a day, when time permitted. Though not tall, Edward did spend the previous day hunched over in an attic that didn't quite allow for his full five foot, ten inch frame. Edward certainly didn't relish the thought of going back up there again today. Maybe take the day off and just relax he told himself. Go through some of the stuff in his father's room. Maybe in the basement too, where it likely would be cooler. Plenty of other things he could do rather than spend the day sweltering in the upper reaches of the house.

Edward went into his parent's master bathroom and grabbed a handful of Advil from the medicine cabinet. "Getting old before my time" he chuckled to himself. To wash down the pain reliever, he leaned over and drank in some cool water, directly from the bathroom faucet. Breakfast was next on his mind. Knowing that he hadn't done any grocery shopping since hastily getting into town the day before his father's death, Edward decided to head back over to the Old Country Kitchen. He figured since the fried chicken from last night was so good, the breakfast ought to be as equally satisfying.

Dressed casually in khaki cargo shorts, a short sleeve, blue pinstriped, buttoned down shirt, and flip flops, Edward figured he'd drive to the restaurant since the heat index was already approaching the low 90's. No sense having to change clothes soaked from sweat just from walking, he thought. He got into his 4-door Black Jeep Wrangler and even before the vehicle's air conditioning had a chance to do its job, he pulled into a parking spot just under the red neon "OPEN" sign on the side of the building.

Pulling open the front door of the restaurant, Edward was pleased with the rush of cold air that smacked him in the face as he approached the hostess stand. From behind, Edward was greeted with a very pleasant "Good morning. Table for one?"

It was Katie, the hostess from last night. "Why, yes Katie, one is just fine." Edward answered.

Just then, another familiar voice rang out from the front door as the bell rang, announcing the guest's arrival. "Make that two Katie. That is if you don't mind sharing a table with ol' Capt'n Petey my boy."

"I sure wouldn't mind at all," Edward replied. "I would enjoy the company. Make that a table for two Katie, please."

As the hostess, Edward and ol' Capt'n Petey made their way to the table, Edward asked Katie if she ever got any time off. "You were hostessing last night. You're back in this morning."

"I wish I got time off!" Katie replied, almost loud enough for the entire dining room to hear. "But this is a family run diner and all us kids are expected to work, to keep it running."

It turns out that Katie's family had been citizens of Bath for as long as anyone could remember. Seems like they've been here as long as the town itself has. Her great-grandfather opened the place back in the 40's. Prior to that, they had all been fisherman. Now they cook other people's catches.

As Katie handed Edward and Captain Petey their menus she informed them that biscuits and sausage gravy with 2 eggs prepared any way you like was on special for $6.99. And the 3 egg western omelet with hash browns and choice of meat was on special for $7.99. And as always, the coffee was on the house. She added, "I'll give you two some time to look over the menu. My brother Hunter will be your server today. He'll be along shortly to bring you water and coffee and to take your order."

“Well Capt’n Petey, you know better than I. What do you suggest?” Edward asked.

“Aye, my boy. Can’t go wrong with nothin’ here, that’s fer sure. Reckon this old sea salt is gonna go with the sausage gravy special.”

Bringing a pot of coffee to the table and dropping water glasses in front of the diners, Hunter, seemingly in a hurry as the dining room started filling up quickly, looked to the old sea captain and asked “the usual Capt’n Petey?’

“No me boy. Reckon the old capt’n will go with the sausage gravy special this mornin’. Sunny side up on the eggs if you please. Sometimes a body just can’t face oatmeal again for breakfast.” Glancing at Edward, with a wink, the captain continued, “truth is, I think that doctor is tryin’ to kill ol’ Capt’n Petey with all this oatmeal in the mornin’.”

Now looking over to Edward, Hunter asked, “And you sir?”

“I have to say Hunter, Capt’n Petey makes a compelling argument. I was just going to get the fruit plate, but what the heck, give me the western omelet special with some of that center cut ham as the meat. And the check too. Make sure I get the check please.”

“Very good sir. Your breakfasts will be along shortly.”

As Hunter turned and walked toward the kitchen to put in the breakfast order Captain Petey said softly to Edward, “Boy, now the old capt’n, he ain’t got much, but he ain’t no charity case neither. I can afford to buy my own breakfast, but I do thank ya kindly.”

“I didn’t mean to insinuate that you couldn’t afford it capt’n. I’m sorry! I, well...., I know you were a friend to my dad after my mother died. Better friend than I was it seems. It’s the least I can do. So thank you for that!”

“Sonny, you don’t have to thank the ol’ capt’n. It was more yer paw bein’ a friend to me rather than the other way ‘round. When I couldn’t captain ships no more and was feelin’ kind a’ low about it, it was your paw that perked up my spirits. He had me out to the house and we played checkers all day, maybe watch the Braves out of Atlanta on the tv. No, it was your paw that deserves the thankin’. Not me.”

“Just the same,” Edward added, “you gave him something to live for once mom and I were gone from the house.”

More to himself than to Edward, the capt’n said very softly, “maybe so. Maybe so.”

Just then, Hunter returned to the table checking on the water glasses. Since they seemed full, he simply said “breakfast will be out shortly gentlemen” as he moved quickly onto the next table.

“Capt’n Petey, I told you yesterday I am here for a while trying to figure some things out. You said you might know what those things might be, though you were pretty cryptic about it….”

“Cryptic? Sorry, this ol’ sea capt’n, he don’t know all them fancy words you college kids use. Don’t rightly know what yer sayin’.”

“I mean you were, I don’t know, like, mysterious, I guess.”

“Aye me boy. I might have been at that, but I made certain promises to your paw and now ain’t the right time for that. Even if that means no free biscuits and gravy neither.”

Edward, now visibly frustrated, decided to change the subject. He picked up his black coffee and took a very slow, careful sip from the piping hot cup. He set it back down on the table before saying, "Capt'n, I couldn't sleep last night. Too many thoughts rushing through my mind. Plus there was that loud storm and then, I was startled by some sort of bright light that came shining through my bedroom window."

Also, picking up his coffee and taking a loud slurp from the cup, Capt'n Petey replied, "Aye lad. I wondered if you'd seen the light from old Capt'n Teach. Don't surprise me none that it came a callin' just followin' your paw's funeral."

"Why do you say that?"

"Just one of the things you'll have to learn on your own, I reckon. But you keep goin' through yer paw's stuff. In time I reckon it will all make sense."

Edward didn't realize that going through the clutter in the attic would lead to any revelations. He had simply been doing it as a means to clean out the house to ready it for what?.....Sale maybe? Edward wasn't quite sure yet what he was going to do with the place. With him now living on the beach up in Nags Head and his parents gone, it didn't make any sort of financial sense to hold onto it. But it was his family's house for decades, it would be hard to just let strangers move into his parent's bedroom and claim it as their own.

Edward's thoughts were quickly interrupted as Hunter once again approached the table, this time with two huge plates of food. While Edward thanked Hunter for the food delivery, the old captain wasted no time attacking his plate. That is, after he dumped a huge amount of hot sauce on top of the eggs which were already on top of the biscuits and gravy.

Edward, eager to find out more of what Captain Petey might know, allowed the captain to eat a sizable portion of his breakfast before trying another angle.

“Good food, eh capt’n?” Edward started.

“Mighty fine boy. Mighty fine,” the captain replied between bites of his biscuit.

“Capt’n, tell me more about this light I saw last night. I suspect you’ve seen it before.”

“Sure have laddie. First time I reckon I was pert near 18. In fact, my birthday was just a few days away. I was first mate on fishing charter here in town. We’d run half and whole day runs up to the Roanoke River or down to the Pamlico and Albemarle. We’d go after Speckled Trout, Spanish Mackerel, Blues, Flounder and Striped Bass, stuff like that.” Using the thermos pitcher of coffee that Hunter left on the table, the captain took this opportunity to top off his cup. He then leaned back took a long sip. And then another. All the while keeping Edward in suspense. He always had that theatrical side to him, the captain would often hear people say.

After a minute or two, the captain continued his thoughts. “Reckon it was late September, hurrikin’ season, you know. But we didn’t have no fancy Dodger Radar or nothin’…”

“Doppler.”

“How’s that boy?”

It’s Doppler Radar” Edward said, trying to be helpful.

"Well, whatever fancy name they call it. We just knowed on our own when foul weather was headin' in. As I was sayin', we just got back from a day on the water and we started to get a big blow outta the nor'east. We'd be feelin' it build all day, but 'specially got worse in the late afternoon. Now the boat owner, a feller named Tommy Boy Owens, he tied up the boat real secure like down at Handy's Point, just south of Bonner's Point. Even though he secured it real good, Mr Owens, he wanted to stay with the boat overnight during the storm, but he had a wife at home who was feelin' kinda poorly. He didn't want to leave her all night in case she be needin' somethin' neither, so he asks me to stay on the boat."

"Weren't you scared staying on that boat during bad weather?" Edward wanted to know.

"Boy, ascared ain't the word fer it. I was down right spooked! I ain't never spent the night on a boat in a Nor'easter before. And this was a big one!"

"I bet," Edward offered up.

"So, I git myself all settled into the wheelhouse. Figured I'd try to sleep in the captain's chair that night. It got to be somewhere after midnight, I know'd that 'cause I heard the church bell ringin' through the howlin' of the wind. Had to be blowin' near gale..."

"Maybe it was the wind blowing that church bell and not that it was midnight."

"I reckon not sonny. I counted them rings when they started."

Just then, Hunter approached the table once again. After being assured that nothing else was needed, he said he'd be back with the check.

The captain continued, “as I was a sayin’ boy, it was just past midnight, the boat was really rockin’, almost couldn’t hold onto to my seat when I saw this big ball of fire down the creek. Looked like it was goin’ back and forth ‘tween the two points. Back and forth from Plum Point across the creek to Archbell Point and back again. Big ball of fire she was, bigger than yer head my boy. Just goin’ back and forth and not even be blowin’ off track by the Nor’easter. Scariest thing I ever did see.”

“I’m sure. You must have been terrified!. Did anyone ever say what it was?”

“No me boy. But you’d been here long ‘nuf. You growed up here. You know’d it was the ghost of ol’ Capt’n Teach himself. Watchin’. Guardin’, over his place north of Teach’s gut. They say his treasure is still there and he be watchin’ over it while searchin’ fer his head.”

“I’ve heard those stories too Capt’n Petey, but come on! They’re just stories… folklore. None of that stuff is true!”

“You might think that sonny. But tell the old capt’n this, what was it you be seein’ last night?”

“I’m not sure capt’n, but I will be making some calls this morning about it. See if anyone else saw it, or had an explanation for it.”

“You can try lad, but all you’d find out is that it was the Light of Ol’ Blackbeard hiself.”

Hunter returned with check in hand. Edward grabbed it, did some mental math in his head for the tip. Figuring 20% to be around $3.00, Edward left a $5 bill on the table. He held out his hand to offer a goodbye to Capt'n Petey, who in turn thanked him for a mighty fine breakfast. Edward got up from the table and headed for the hostess stand to pay. As he did, he grabbed onto Petey's shoulder and told him that he would let him know about his findings on last night's light. As he did, he heard Petey say "sure you will my boy. Sure you will...."

At the hostess stand, Edward handed Katie a twenty dollar bill, waited for his change, then opened the door, once again ringing the bell atop it, and walked out into the oppressive heat of the day.

Chapter 5

Back at home, Edward had the six window air conditioners spread throughout the house going full-blast in hopes of staving off the heat and humidity of the day. But Mother Nature was winning that battle. After brushing his teeth to get rid of the coffee taste in his mouth, Edward sat down on the couch, right below the air conditioning unit in the living room window. He had with him the book he had started the night before, "*The Pyrates and Buccaneers of the Carolinas*."

Rather than reading about them all, Edward jumped ahead to the chapter on Blackbeard. It told the story of the English Pyrate (as the book spelled it) as he roamed the West Indies and the eastern coast of the North American colonies. It told how Blackbeard, likely from the seaport of Bristol, England, started out as a sailor on privateer ships during Queen Anne's War. The war was basically the second edition of the French and Indian War fought between England and France for control over North America. In fact, Blackbeard had captured a French merchant vessel and re-named her "Queen Anne's Revenge." It further went on to describe the blockade of Charles Town Harbor in the Province of South Carolina. Holding an entire city hostage for much needed medicines. It also told of Blackbeard's final battle and eventual death at the crafty hands of Lieutenant Robert Maynard. All things that Edward had already known about the pirate, who lived hundreds of years ago, just down the street from where he now sat.

But there were a couple things Edward had never heard before. While it was common knowledge that in 1718 the pirate captain settled in Bath and married Mary Ormond after taking the Crown's pardon. What wasn't previously known was that ol' Blackbeard and Mary had a son at some point. A son who seemingly just drifted into history's oblivion. Other than Blackbeard's son's birth, nothing else was mentioned. The other interesting fact discovered by Edward was that there was also some confusion as to the pirate's actual name. Commonly Blackbeard had been referred to as Edward Teach, but this source indicates that it may very well have been Edward Thatch. A name very similar to his own, Edward Thatcher!

What did this all mean Edward wondered as he wiped the sweat accumulating on his forehead, the ac unit, not doing its job. Is this what his father had wanted to impart upon him all these years? Maybe, just maybe, they were direct descendants of the black-hearted pirate captain? It really couldn't be that. Could it?

Edward got up from the couch and very gently put down the book, treating it now as a family heirloom, rather than just an old musty, dusty book found in a random steamer trunk in the attic. Is that what Capt'n Petey Dussault meant when he said at breakfast that it was fitting that last night's appearance of "Teach's Light" showed itself just after Edward Senior's funeral. No. He couldn't believe that. Edward just didn't believe in such nonsense. In fact he was going to prove that last night's light has a true scientific explanation.

Edward went back upstairs to his bedroom, where it was even hotter then the rooms on the first level of the house. The window air conditioners tried their best, but they were fighting a losing battle with the heat building further outside. In his closet, Edward retrieved his backpack which held his laptop computer. He also grabbed a pen and the reporter's notebook that he always carried. No self respecting journalist would ever be without one.

Back downstairs he went and spread his work items out on the kitchen table, bound and determined to prove once and for all, that the random light from last night wasn't the ghost of Captain Teach, or as Edward now knew him, Captain Thatch.

Edward opened his laptop and hit the on/off button to fire it up. Once on, he typed in his wireless password. On the last visit Edward had made to his dad's house, he missed a big news story about a huge drug bust in his new hometown of Nags Head. A huge cocaine smuggling ring was being closely monitored by the Dare County Sheriff's Department until they were able to gather enough evidence against those involved. Then out of nowhere in the early morning hours, the County Sheriff's Department working with the State Police and Federal ATF agents, surrounded a house just to the north of where Edward lived and took all involved into custody. Frustrated by not being able to write the story remotely from his father's house, Edward had set up a wireless network, vowing to never miss a story again just because he was visiting what Edward called the 1970's, or what his dad referred to simply as "home."

On his computer Edward pulled up the non-emergency number for the Bath, North Carolina Police Department.

As the second ring faded, and just before the start of the third ring, Edward heard: "Bath Police, Chief Haney speaking." It was Pat Haney, Bath's Police Chief for at least the last two decades. He had been appointed to that position by Mayor Wheeler and has remained as such through 3 different mayors now. Each new mayor never wanting to be the one to replace the very popular police chief.

"Hi Chief Haney. This is Edward Thatcher. My parents, until recently, have lived over on King Street."

"Yes Mr Thatcher. I was sorry to hear about your paw. Your maw too. They were both wonderful people. A real asset to our town. How may I help?"

"Well Chief, as you no doubt already know, I'm in town from Nags Head, where I now live. I'm trying to figure out what to do with my parent's house."

"Newspaperman, am I right?"

"Magazine actually, but yeah. I have kind of a weird question for you...."

"Go ahead son...."

"Last night, some time before 2 am or so, did the department get any reports of anything weird?"

"Weird meaning what exactly?" The police chief asked

"Well, I don't exactly know how to explain this," Edward replied. "I guess anything like strange lights or something. Did you get any reports on something like that?"

"Well son," the chief said. "Nothing out of the ordinary. Now it was blustery and there was a lot of lightening and thunder last night. Maybe what you saw was lightening."

"No chief. This was more of a constant light that went back and forth across Bath Creek from what looked like Plum Point to Archbell Point. It never wavered off-track, not even with last night's strong winds."

"Now son, you know what you're describing don't ya?"

"Yes chief, I do. As a matter of fact I had this same conversation with an old sea captain over breakfast this morning at the Old Country Kitchen, but I can't..." Edward paused for a moment, taking a sip from the bottle of water he had sitting next to his computer before continuing on. "I can't hardly believe this light I saw was that of Old Captain Blackbeard."

There was quiet on the other end of the telephone for what felt like a very uneasy 10 seconds or so before the Bath Police Chief spoke. “Well Mr Thatcher, being a sensible man, I also don’t know what you’re describing is that of a ghost of a pirate that lived here some 300 hundred years ago. But I can tell you this, I have been in this town for longer than you’ve been alive I expect. I haven’t yet found any other plausible explanation for it. I reckon the town pays it very little attention anymore, and just accepts it as face value of it being Blackbeard. In fact, yours is the first call this department has taken about it in at least a dozen years. People here in Bath just take it as something that is part of the town.”

Edward not really satisfied with this answer continued. “What about your patrolman on duty last night. Nothing in his report from his shift?”

“I will be honest with you son. I did read his report and there was mention of the storm, the downed branches on the outskirts of town and he did simply write “Teach was back.” But nothing more than that and certainly nothing I needed further explanation on. Like I said, just part of the town’s fabric now.”

Very disappointed that his first call didn’t put to rest this “Teach’s Light nonsense,” Edward simply said “Thanks for your time Chief. Have a great day!”

“You too Mr Thatcher. And son? I truly am sorry for your recent loss. Both Pam and Ed Sr., they were real nice folks.”

Edward Jr. thanked the chief for his kind words and clicked off the call.

In the reporter's notebook Edward drew a line through the words "Police Department." The next item on his list was the National Weather Service. Edward did some checking on the internet and found that Bath was served by the National Weather Service Office in Morehead City, North Carolina. In addition to a phone number the office also had an email address. Already feeling a little weird about his discussion with Chief Haney, Edward decided to email his question.

Dear Madam or Sir,

My name is Edward Thatcher. Currently I am in Bath, NC, and as I understand it, the Morehead office services this area.

Last night I experienced something that may have been a weather phenomenon and was hoping you could shed some further light on it (no pun intended). Somewhere between 1 and 2 am, I was at Bonner's Point looking southward. What I saw was a constant light. When I say constant, I mean that it always glowed. It didn't flash like the lightening that was also present. This light kept traveling basically east to west and then west to east, back and forth across Bath Creek. Can you provide any information as to what this was please?

Thank you!

Before hitting send, Edward put his name in the Bcc line so he had a copy of what he was sending to the National Weather Service. Just a few short minutes later, Edward received an email in his in-box from the Weather Service indicating that they received his inquiry and they would be contacting him shortly.

Knowing that it may take a day or two before he'd receive a response, Edward moved on the third item he had neatly printed on his list. Wesley Walker. Wesley was an old high school friend of Edward's. They played baseball together and swam on the same swim teams. Though not close friends currently, they have maintained an on-line friendship via Facebook and LinkedIn. Each keeping tabs on the other's success. While Edward moved to the Outer Banks to start his magazine, Wesley moved over to be a news reader for "Little Washington AM 1100," the number one rated news station in the area. Wesley, in the ensuing years had made his way to the top of the news perch at the station by being named its News Director about 5 years ago. Edward knew that Wesley would know of the "Teach Light" folklore, but would also be the one to not believe in it. Ever since they were little kids, it was Wesley who never believed anything he couldn't touch, see, or feel. In fact, Wesley was the first agnostic that Edward had ever met. Not an atheist mind you, but an agnostic. He never said there wasn't a God like an atheist would, but rather holds the opinion that something like existence of God is unknown or unknowable. Not a popular belief when you live in the actual buckle of the Bible Belt.

Edward shot a quick direct message to Wesley via Facebook, letting his friend know that he was in town briefly and if available would like to meet for lunch in the next day or two. Almost immediately, the tone on Edward's laptop rang, indicating that he had a message come in from Facebook. In the message, Wesley said that he was free today and to meet him at East Coast Wings and Grill over on W. 15th, just down the street from the Washington Square Mall between 1 and 1:30pm.

Glancing up at the wall, still full from his 3-egg omelet from just an hour ago, Edward was glad to see he still had nearly four hours before having to worry about eating again. Being back "home" in Bath hasn't done much for his waistline Edward chuckled to himself.

With some time to kill, Edward decided to walk off some of his breakfast by returning to the spot that he found himself in the wee hours of the morning. The bench in the park at Bonner's Point. He didn't know what he hoped to find there, but felt the need to go back nonetheless.

He stepped out onto the front porch of the house into weather he could only describe as "soupy." The air was heavy with water vapor. The sun was hot. The air temperature had to be north of 90 by now with the "feels like" temp nearing triple digits. Edward was happy the walk was only about a half-mile. No way he would have made it otherwise.

Just a few minutes later he stood in front of the Bonner House, the white wood framed house, built in 1820 that stood across Front Street from the park. From there he went back down to the water's edge and climbed a tree to the right of the bench where he was perched just 8 hours ago. He looked out onto Bath Creek. The sun, reflecting down onto the blue ripples of the water, shot back points of light that momentarily blinded Edward. He had to bring his right hand up to shade his eyes from the sun, his left hand, holding onto the trunk of the tree. He looked south toward the direction of Plum Point, the piece of land that extends furthest into the creek. He could see nothing out of the ordinary. Only three boats out fishing and a couple of jet skiers enjoying the coolness of the water on this otherwise stifling hot day. A completely different scene than was there just last night.

Just as Edward was about to climb down from his perch in the tree, he was startled by a voice.

"Mister, what are you doing, standing in that tree?" Came a voice from a preteen little blonde haired girl in shorts and a Bath Elementary School t-shirt.

"Oh, nothing. Just looking down the creek." Edward answered.

"Well, you better be careful mister. My brother Ethan fell out of that tree last month and broke his arm. And he wasn't even as old and as fat as you are."

Not taking a liking to the description the little girl saw of him, Edward replied back, "thanks for the advice. I'm just climbing down now."

Just then Edward heard a voice yelling "Elise! Come back here now!" With that, the little girl turned and ran back to her family, which included what looked like a young teenager with a cast on his left arm. "I guess I do look pretty out of place, a full grown man climbing a tree," Edward thought to himself.

After making his way back to the ground, carefully, for he didn't want to have the same experience as poor Ethan, Edward walked over to the last remaining vacant picnic table in the shade. He sat there, sweat now dripping from his forehead into his eyes, stinging just a bit. Edward suddenly felt all alone. His mother was gone. His dad just died. It's a pretty silly thought that being in his mid-thirties that he identifies himself as being an orphan. At what age are you too old to be considered an orphan? 18? 21? Certainly by the time you're 34. Edward sat there a good long time under the shade of the tree contemplating Teach's Light, the significance of the closeness of his name to that of a bloodthirsty pirate, and certainly not the least of which, what it was that Capt'n Petey knew that he didn't. The things that Edward's dad had to say just days prior to passing away. And what was he going to do with the house? All questions that seemingly had no immediate answer. At least none that he knew of.

Edward pulled his cell phone out of the back pocket of his shorts to check in with his office in Nags Head. He dialed the number and before the first ring even completed ringing, his secretary answered.

"Milepost 11 Publishing. Char speaking."

“Hey Char. It's Edward. Just had a few minutes so I thought I'd check in to see if anything needed my attention.”

“Oh, hey boss. No, I don't think so. Billy is out talking to the director of the Theater of Dare this morning. Talking to them about their upcoming season. Sounds like they will be putting on several productions this year.”

Billy was a recent grad from The Ohio State University School of Journalism and was hired to write feature articles and to sell some ad space as well. Though he's only been with the magazine for less than a year, he's already proven his worth by uncovering a big story having to do with a mega-gift shop wanting to break ground in several towns on the Outer Banks. It would have been a move that would have put several of the mom and pop shops out of business. The story rallied the local townspeople to pressure those in a position to do so, to turn the huge corporation down from building on the beach. That story by itself increased circulation nearly 10%.

“Great!” Edward replied. “That should make for a good story. Remind him too, to look for a statement from the folks at the Lost Colony. See how they're helping promote the smaller theater company.”

“Will do boss. Anything else?”

Edward paused for a moment. Not sure that what he wanted to ask, should be asked.

“Boss, you still there?”

“Yeah, sorry Char. How busy is it there right now?”

“Not too bad. I got it all handled. I'm re-upping some advertisers for the next issue, getting together “Letters to the Editor” and I'm putting together my profile of local author Joseph L.S. Terrell. He has a new book about to be released. Why, what's up?”

Drawing in a deep breath, Edward continued "well, if you have time, I have a little research project I'd like you to look into."

"Sure boss. This for the upcoming issue?"

"May not be for any issue. It may just be for my own personal use. I haven't decided yet. So don't make it your top priority, just look at in your spare time."

"Ok, whatcha got?"

"Blackbeard. I want you to put together a quick report on the pirate captain for me. Most specifically I'd like to know more about the folklore surrounding the phenomenon known as "Teach's Light" and the derivation of his name. See if you can find out anything about him having a kid also, will ya?"

"Back home in Bath got you thinking about doing a book on the town's most infamous resident?" Char asked.

"No Char, nothing like that. At least I don't think so anyway. Let's just call it, satisfying my own curiosity about something."

"Got it boss. When do you want this by?"

"Not real pressing. Take care of the magazine first. If you get to it, you get to it. I'm hoping to be back sometime next week, so just hold it there for me if you get to it before then."

"You got it boss. Again, I'm very sorry about your dad. You doing ok?"

"Yeah. I'm good Char. I just learned a bit too late that some things needed to be done and said. Have a good day Char."

"You too boss. You too." With that both sides disconnected their side of the call. Char put the phone down a little sadder than she was just a few minutes ago. Edward had been a good boss, though they never could be classified as good friends, she now felt sad for the things he seemed to be going through. She decided right there that she would have that report for Edward when he returned, even if it meant she would have to work on it during her free time over the weekend.

Edward too, feeling sad, checked the time, slipped the cellphone back into his back pocket and started for home to take a shower before having to meet up with Wesley Walker in Little Washington.

Chapter 6

It was about 1:15 as Edward pulled into the parking lot of East Coast Wings and Grill. He had never been to this location, but had visited their restaurant in Mount Airy, North Carolina, on Andy Griffith Parkway; coincidentally when Edward was doing a story for his magazine on the actor and his early beginnings. The gauge on the Jeep's dashboard indicating the outside temperature was now a blistering 97 degrees. Reason enough for the outside patio on the side of the white bricked building to be empty. Even people accustomed to the summer heat sought out the comfort of the inside air conditioning.

As soon as Edward walked in to take his place in line at the hostess stand to be seated, he felt a slap on his back.
"Well if it ain't my ol' buddy, buddy Edward the famous magazine tycoon up there on the Outer Banks."

It was Wesley. It had to be Wesley, Edward thought, as he turned quickly and came eye-to-eye with his old high school friend. Dressed in a pair of Khaki's, the type with the stretch material that allowed Wesley to pull them up over his now ample belly. Tucked into the khakis was a turquoise East Coast Wings golf shirt. Judging not only by his wardrobe, but by his physique too, it appeared Wesley spent a great deal of time at this wing place.

"Wesley you old so and so. How are you? Haven't seen you in ages!" Edward bellowed.

"Yeah pert near 15 years, I'd expect Edward." I already have a table in the back. Let's go sit down and tell each other some lies." With that, Edward followed Wesley to the back section of the restaurant. Wesley already had a Budweiser on the table.

"Starting early I see, Wes" Edward said as he motioned to the beer.

"Early? Not hardly! It's going on 1:30 in the afternoon. I start my day at the radio station at 5 am. My day's about over."

Wesley motioned for the server. Coming to the table almost immediately, a young, blonde girl of about 22 dressed in black shorts that came tastefully to top of her knees. She also wore a white t-shirt imprinted with a get your "screaming beaver" BBQ sauce at East Coast Wings.

"Hi, I'm Brittney. Can I start you off with a beverage? Water? Sweet Tea? Beer?"

"Hi Brittney," Edward said, I'll stick with a sweet tea please."

"Yes sir." Turning her attention to Wesley, "Mr Walker, you ok? You need another Bud?"

"Nah, darlin', I'm good for now."

With that, Brittney turned and started for the bar area to retrieve a glass of the sweet tea for Edward.

"Sorry to hear about your pop" Wesley said. "He was a good dude."

"Thanks." Edward replied.

"Sorry I couldn't make the funeral, but me and Mary, we had the kids out to see her folks in Virginia and couldn't get back in time."

"No worries Wes. It's fine. I can't expect you to drop your family to make it. It's fine, really."

Just then Brittney made it back to the table and set down Edward's sweet tea in front of him. On a saucer, she also brought a few extra lemon slices.

"You gentlemen ready to order?" Asked Brittney. "Boneless wings are on special. Sixty-five cents each."

"Lunch is on me, ol' buddy" Wesley piped in. "Well, actually the radio station. I'll write it off as a business luncheon."

“Thanks Wes, but you don’t have to do that…”

“I insist, ol’ buddy. Now don’t make Brittney stand there and wait on you any longer than she has to. She’s got other tables to attend to.”

“Well, ok then. Thanks to the radio station.” Thinking back to his run in at Bonner Point with little Elise, the young girl that called him fat, Edward decided to go with the Cobb Salad. “Dressing on the side please.”

“Very good sir” as Brittney turned her attention to Wesley as the news director mumbled something about “salads being for girls.”

“Your usual, Mr Walker?”

“Yes Brittney, if you please. Let me get 15 boneless wings with the “screaming beaver sauce” and a basket of fries. Might as well throw another Budweiser on that too.”

“Yes sir Mr. Walker. Coming right up!” And with that, Brittney headed over to the server station to place the order.

With the order placed and beverages on the table, it was Wesley who spoke first. “Ok ol’ buddy. Was is it?”

Caught a little off-guard by the question, Edward replied with a simple “huh?”

“You didn’t ask to meet me for lunch just for old times sake. It’s been 15 years, why lunch now? See, my old news instincts tell me you need something.”

Sheepishly, Edward agreed that it wasn’t just a social lunch. “You got me there Wes. Yes, there is a reason I wanted to have a lunch with you.”

“I knew it!” Pointing to his nose, Wesley said, “this thing can smell out news every time. It has never failed me once.”

"Well, it's not exactly news that I wanted to talk about. I'm not really sure how to phrase it exactly,"

Wesley picked up the Budweiser bottle, took a long pull from it, put the bottle back on the table, now nearly empty, and said, "just take your time ol' buddy. Start at the beginning."

"Well, ok. Here it goes. I wanted to talk with you, because you're the one guy who doesn't accept anything that you haven't been able to prove."

"Uh-huh. If I can't see it, touch it or feel it, it doesn't exist."

"Right. That's what I remembered most about you." Edward added. "Now last night I was staying in my parent's house...."

"Yeah, the big white one on King Street. I remember the place."

"Yeah. So I was in bed and this big storm comes rumbling through..."

"Yeah, we got the same storm here in Little Washington last night too..." Wesley said.

"I'm sure you did Wes. But there was more to it than just that. Somewhere at about 2am or so, this bright light was shining..."

"Sure it wasn't just lightening?"

"No. It was different than lightening" Edward continued. "This was a constant light that moved across the creek, east to west.....then west to east. Never wavering from its path. Not by rain. Not by wind."

Looking at his friend closely and picking up his beer, Wesley downed the last of the Bud, just as Brittney returned with a replacement bottle and to top off Edward's sweet tea.

“You do know what you’re describing, don’t ‘cha ol’ buddy?” Wesley answered.

“Yeah. I know. Teach’s Light. But there’s got to be a real answer to this. Not just some fable. You don’t believe in fables, and neither do I.”

Picking up his second Budweiser and taking a sip off it, Wesley continued. “Here’s what I can tell you about that ol’ buddy. Like you, I don’t believe in the folklore of Teach’s Light. I did a news story on it for the radio station about 6 or 7 years ago. Even channel 7 here in town carried the story. I talked to the police chief in town….”

“Chief Haney.”

“Yeah, Chief Haney. Why, you know him?”

“Not really. I talked to him this morning about what I saw. He just brushed it off as Teach’s Light. Didn’t really take my call seriously, I don’t think. Said his deputy on duty last night indicated that Teach was back, or something like that, but didn’t have much to say.”

“Pretty much the same response I got from him too” Wesley said. “I also talked with some old sea captain. Said he saw Teach’s Light back when he was a teenager and was mating on some fishing charter.”

“Yeah, that would have been Capt’n Petey. He’s a friend of my dad. I’ve run into him a couple of times.”

“Some eye witness accounts all saying the same thing as you are is all I ever got for the story.” Wesley continued, “I never got a clear-cut answer to this phenomenon we all call Teach’s Light. So if you’re turning to me for answers, well, ol’ buddy, I ain't got none.”

“But you don’t believe in Teach’s Light, do you?” Edward wanted to know.

"Reckon I don't know what I believe at this point. Have you tried the National Weather Service or the folks at the airport?"

"I sent the Weather Service an email. Some robot replied almost immediately that they received my email and someone will get back to me, but nothing as of yet. I hadn't thought of the airport."

"I asked the same questions to the Weather Service and the airport. Pretty much the same answer as Chief Handley…"

"Haney. It's Chief Haney…"

"Whatever. Same answer. People have seen it. People have reported it. But there has been no scientific explanation for it. In fact, it seems that in recent years, people have even stopped reporting it."

It was at this point that Brittney returned to the table. Setting the cobb salad in front of Edward first, with the vinaigrette dressing on the side, and then the wings and fries in front of Wesley, asking if they needed anything else. When she was assured they didn't need anything more, she left, allowing the two men to attack their lunches, which they did, in relative silence, each thinking his own thoughts.

Once the lunch was finished, Wesley grabbed the check and allowed Edward to lay down the tip. As they walked out, it was Wesley who said to Edward, "well, ol' buddy, sorry I didn't have the answers you were looking for. And I'm afraid you're just not going to find them here. I mean, this agnostic has been able to just set it aside and let people just believe it is nothing more than Old Captain Teach guarding his buried treasure down there somewhere near Teach's Gut."

"I don't know Wes. I can't just leave it alone. At least not yet. But thanks for lunch just the same."

"No worries Edward, let's just not wait another 15 years before we do it again!"

"You got it Wes. Thanks again."

The two men went their separate ways in the parking lot, Edward watching what can only be described as Wes "waddling" to his Chevy HHR, with the magnetic "News Radio AM 1100" sign on the driver and passenger doors. Edward walked toward his Jeep. He climbed in and turned the key to start his 20 minute drive down US 264 and 92 back to King Street in Bath.

Chapter 7

Edward spent the next several days going through boxes in the attic when the heat of the day wasn't too intense; boxes in the basement when it was. He went through steamer trunks. He went through his parents' closets. Though there wasn't much left in his mother's. Apparently his dad had already taken care of that task sometime after her passing. A lonely task that his father likely had to do on his own. That thought once again caused Edward to feel guilty for not being around more for his dad after his mother had died.

The only thing Edward Sr. had left hanging in Pam's closest was the wedding dress she had worn some 40 odd years ago. On the floor were her wedding shoes. On the shelf above where the clothes hung, the wedding album full of black and white pictures.

Those items Edward packed up very carefully and put aside to take back to Nags Head. What he was going to do with them he didn't have a clue. He certainly wasn't going to throw them out with the rest of the trash that was starting to collect on the back porch.

As Edward worked his way through each box and space in the house, he carefully looked at each item to see if that particular thing might bring him closer to the answers he was seeking. What was it that his father wanted to impart to him? What was it that Capt'n Petey knew that Edward didn't?

In fact, wanting to talk to the captain further, Edward had made a few more meal runs to the Old Country Kitchen the last several days, never running into him. Hostess Katie even remarked that she hadn't seen the old sea captain in a while, which wasn't normal.

Returning home after another, way too much food kind of meal, Edward pulled the Jeep to the back of the house. He noticed the slumping mounds of trash on the back porch and decided to take it out to the street. What was today anyway? Monday? Tuesday? He wasn't sure. Without the structure of work everyday, each day just slipped into the next. He did, however, notice the neighbors had already taken their trash out, so garbage day was probably the next day.

As Edward struggled to carry each box and bag to the curb he noticed the winds picking up. There were also thick, black low-hanging clouds to the northeast. The direction of his house back on the Outer Banks in Nags Head. Having not received a satisfactory answer from the National Weather Center in Morehead City, only that they had no real explanation for what Edward saw that night close to a week ago, Edward decided that he'd start back for home the next day. He needed to get back to the magazine since the next issue was due to be released soon. He'd wait for the garbage men to come by first so he could stow the cans away before leaving town. As Edward hauled the last can to the curb, he noticed the temperature had dropped significantly.

Back in the house, Edward went back to looking through some papers he had found in his father's desk. It seemed this hobby of his, playing Blackbeard, for schools, fairs and corporate events was a bit more than just a hobby. Edward Sr. had compiled quite a stack of research on the old pirate captain. Where he'd been. What he had done. Any acquaintances he might of had. Edward Sr. seemed especially curious of whatever became of Mary Ormond; Mrs Blackbeard, and their son Edward. There were copies of old journals from Bristol, England. Edward Sr. had apparently contacted a museum there and they were kind enough to send copies of the journal. Junior wondering what kind of story Senior concocted to get them to send these copies. There were also books, stacks of legal pads, all with his father's handwriting all over them. Lots of speculations and questions. Very few answers. There was an entry that Edward Jr. had found recounting a story of a young Pete Dussault encountering "Teach's Light." A story that Edward Jr. had heard only a few days ago over breakfast. There was another story that had caught the son's attention. This one is Edward Sr. telling his experience of "Teach's Light." His dad's experience was eerily similar to his own. It happened on a storm-filled night. Senior was having trouble sleeping when in his upstairs bedroom the light appeared. As did Junior, Senior threw on some clothes and went out into the night toward Bonner Point and watched the light travel over Bath Creek in a constant East-West, West-East direction without wavering from the weather conditions.

Chapter 8

With the rain pelting the house and the winds blowing hard against the windows, causing them to rattle in their frames, Edward read late into the night. So late in fact, that he found himself hunched over the desk the next morning. At some point he had fallen asleep at the desk. He stood up very slowly. Sleeping in the chair did not do his back any favors as he tried to stretch the kinks out of it. He thought that maybe a hot shower would help with the aching muscles so he went upstairs to the bathroom.

Edward stood under the hot water for quite a while that morning for two reasons. One, he was trying to soak his back muscles back to normal. And secondly, he found he did some of his best thinking in the shower. He didn't know why that was, maybe it had something to do with it being a monotonous task that allows his unconscious mind to free up for a creative epiphany. Edward had heard of others having similar experiences while fishing or exercising. His creative juices, for whatever reason, kicked in when he was in the shower.

While allowing the hot water to fall onto his head and down his shoulders and ultimately down to his feet, Edward thought again about his father's papers. The research, the encounters with Teach's Light. All of it. Unfortunately nothing had come together for him. As the water starting slowly, and then more rapidly, change from hot to warm to lukewarm, Edward figured he'd better dry off and get dressed. He'd stop at the Old Country Kitchen again for breakfast hoping to catch up with Capt'n Petey before leaving town. He also hoped that the trash collectors would come sooner rather than later so he could get on the road for his two plus hour drive back to Nags Head.

As he toweled himself off, Edward looked out of the upstairs bathroom window. The winds still blew fairly hard, bending some of the smaller trees in the neighboring yards. The rain was coming down at a slant. Looked like it would be an interesting drive back to the Outer Banks, he thought. But that was why he always drove a Jeep Wrangler.

Edward got himself dressed in a pair of cargo shorts, a UNC - Chapel Hill t-shirt and flip flops as he made his way out of the house and into the Jeep for the short ride to breakfast. Instantly he was struck as to how cold it had become. Just a few days ago it was in the 90's. Upper 90's at that. Now the temperature on the Jeep's dashboard showed a very chilly 46.

As Edward turned left onto Carteret Street, heading to what had become his only meal place while in town, he noticed the garbage trucks were just a few houses down from his own. Unfortunately for them, the weather making their job much more difficult that morning. Fortunately for Edward, however, was that they would have collected all his trash by the time he finished his breakfast, so he would be able to close up the house and head back to Nags Head right after eating.

Edward passed the post office on the right. The Bath Fire Station on the left, and as he did so, he noticed that one of the doors were up and one truck missing. Apparently on a run of some sort. Across the street was the Family Dollar and then the Old Country Kitchen on the left. Edward pulled into the lot and ran for the front door, ringing it's bell as he pulled the door of the diner open.

Not surprisingly, Katie was at her post and immediately took Edward to one of the many vacant tables that morning. He assumed the inclement weather was keeping diners away. Katie once again mentioned to Edward that Capt'n Petey had not been in and was a bit worried about him. They had thought to check up on him, but no one knew quite where he lived.

Since it was a slow morning, Katie pulled double duty as hostess and server. She brought Edward his black, unsweetened coffee and took his order of biscuits and gravy with a side of hash browns. Edward not caring about the "fat"comment from Elise from several days ago.

The food was brought to him quickly and he consumed it equally as quick. He left Katie a $5 tip on a $9.75 check. Once he paid his bill, he left Katie his card and asked her or Capt'n Petey to call him once the ol' captain popped up again. She agreed that she would.

Edward pushed open the glass door and ran for the Jeep. The rain still coming down in a slant and the wind howling. Looking up in the sky he knew there would be no sun to warm up this day. In fact, a quick check at the temperature reading in the Jeep, showed it had dropped another degree. Now down to 45.

Relieved to have found that the garbage men had been by, Edward grabbed the cans and quickly threw them up on the back porch. He knew he would have to secure them somehow since he'd be gone a while, but he first ran into the house to grab an old rain jacket of his father's and threw it on. Edward ran back outside and decided the cans would be better off on the front screened-in porch than secured on the back porch. He threw them there, went back in the house, turned off all lights, made sure all windows were closed and pulled the front door shut and locked it. As he did, Edward couldn't help but think that this was probably the first time in over 40 years that this house had been locked up. In small town North Carolina, it just didn't seem necessary.

Edward hopped into his Jeep to begin his drive back "home" to the Outer Banks. Instead of heading north on King Street, he headed south. South To Craven Street where he took a right. He stopped at St Thomas Episcopal, the brick church built back in 1734. There in the church yard cemetery was fresh dirt that had recently been dug up. Edward got out of the Jeep. The rain, the wind, the cold, not bothering him now as he stood at his parents' plot. The headstone with his mother's name, birth date and death date. His father's name and birth date. The death date not yet chiseled into the granite.

Edward stood there under the branches of a massive oak, that somehow didn't seem vulnerable in the storm. Clearly, Edward thought, this tree had weathered many a storm, she'll do just fine in this one too. Edward said a silent prayer and then promised his dad that he would find out the answers that both father and son were seeking. After a few more minutes and now soaked to the bone, Edward climbed into the Jeep, cranked up the heat and headed north back up King Street, waving as he passed the family home.

Chapter 9

Edward decided to take the southerly route back to the Outer Banks. The one up US 264 through Belhaven, Swan Quarter and Sumpy Point before getting onto US 64 to Roanoke Island and then onto the beach, rather than the northerly route of US 32 to Us 64 through Roper and Creswell. It would take a few minutes longer, but Edward preferred it. Plus the few extra minutes of quiet time wouldn't hurt.

The rain was coming down harder now. The windshield wipers were already going as fast as they could and were struggling to keep up with all the water. The winds were blowing even stronger, coming out of the northeast, pushing the left-front part of the car towards the ditch on the right side of the road. Debris was blowing everywhere and it wasn't long before Edward noticed he was the only car on the road. Though, in this part of North Carolina, that wasn't really an all-together strange thing.

Edward made it across the Pantego Creek and into Belhaven, forty-five minutes after leaving the house. More than double the time that it would normally take. At the corner of Main Street and Route 264, he pulled into the Dunkin' Donuts, ran out of the Jeep and into the front door. Not because he needed a break from the driving just yet, but because he needed a break from the wind and the rain. Hoping that a hot cup of black coffee and a few minutes would give Mother Nature some time to blow herself out.

Belhaven, is not what is considered to be a large town. Maybe 2,000 people or so. And on this cold, rainy, blustery day, it seemed like a ghost town. Edward was greeted by a bored, mid-thirtyish, dirty blonde haired girl whose name tag said her name was Tanya. Tanya no doubt would have preferred to be home rather than tending this totally empty store.

“Howdy, what can I getcha?” Tanya asked Edward as he approached the counter. “Donuts are half-priced right now since the morning rush is over.”

Edward, patting his stomach, remembering the biscuits, sausage gravy and hash browns from this morning’s breakfast, said “Just a large black coffee please.”

As Tanya turned around to pour the coffee from one of two pots on the burners behind her, Edward asked, “So where is everyone this morning?”

“Reckon this blow has everybody stayin’ in today. Stayin’ in and stayin’ warm and dry I expect,” Tanya answered. “Getcha anything else?”

“No thanks. I think I’ll just grab a table and sip on my coffee awhile. Wait and see if this rain lets up a bit before hitting the road back home.”

“Suit yourself. Let me know if you need anything.”

“Thanks, I will.” And with that Edward headed towards a table up against the front window, but not until he stuck a couple of dollars into the tip jar. Realizing that Tanya hadn’t seen him do it, Edward strangely felt like he was in a “Seinfeld” episode. Should he tell her he stuck the bills in there? Should he not? After a short internal struggle he decided to just grab a seat and enjoy his coffee.

After several minutes and no additional customers, Tanya grabbed the coffee pot and headed over to Edward to top off his cup. “On the house,” she said.

“Thanks” Edward replied. “Doesn’t look like this is gonna let up anytime soon, does it?.”

“No, I expect it won’t. Seems kinda ridiculous to keep the place open, but them’s the rules. Whether anyone is here or not, I have to be here.”

"Well, I guess the good news is you'll get paid to just do nothing" Edward said, not knowing what else to say.

Tanya took the pot back to the counter and started filing her nails. Edward stood, asked for a top for his to-go cup and made a mad dash back out to the Jeep.

In the Jeep, again, soaked to the bone, Edward turned on the Bluetooth on his cell phone so he could connect to the "Tune In" app, to listen to Ocean 105 on the Outer Banks. He wanted to see if he could get any up-to-the-minute reports on the weather. He didn't have to wait long before the booming voice of John Clark came through loud and clear.

"Today on the Outer Banks, look for persistent winds out of the Northeast at about 35 miles per hour, gusting to near 50. Rains will continue to pound the Northern Dare beaches, some of it heavy. Look for some of those bands to bring between 1-2 inches of rain per hour. The Red flags are flying folks, so that means no going into the ocean today, but it's too cold for that anyway. The next tide at Oregon Inlet will be a high tide, coming in at 2:11 this afternoon. With the Perigean Tide we can expect heavy beach erosion, so let's be careful out there! Currently in Nags Head, its a very chilly 49 degrees with heavy rain."

Edward knew from past experiences living on the barrier island that the Perigean Tide is not particularly good news in a storm like this. Perigean tides occur a few times a year when the moon, the sun, and the Earth are all aligned. It's called a "spring tide," but has nothing to do with spring. The infamous Ash Wednesday Storm of 1962, which resulted in the loss of 40 lives and $500,000,000 in property damage, coincided with the Perigean spring tide.

Seat belt fastened, Edward put the Jeep into the first of its six gears as he pulled back out onto Route 264. As before, the road was deserted. The stop lights, hanging above intersections, looked like kites, swaying in the wind. But that didn't matter. They were almost invisible anyway due to the amount of rain that was falling. Edward crept along, never really getting the Jeep higher than fourth gear as he continued his journey back to the beach.

A little over an hour later Edward had Lake Mattamsuskeet on his left as he pointed the jeep towards Englehard and then onto Stumpy Point. The rain and the wind never giving up the whole time. It felt like Edward was in a battle with Mother Nature as to whom would be the first to say "uncle." Would she blow herself out and finally be dried up of all rain? Or would Edward finally pull off the road and wait it out? Both hard headed. Both Stubborn. They both challenged the other.

By the time he arrived at the Croatan Sound in Manns Harbor to cross over to Roanoke Island, Edward was relieved to have made the choice of his Southerly route home. While listening to Ocean 105 on the drive, it was announced that the Alligator River Bridge was stuck open and the operator wasn't able to get it back closed again, stranding about a dozen motorists on the bridge. By taking his preferred route from the south, Edward was able to avoid that bridge altogether.

Edward slowly inched his Jeep over the Croatan Sound on the Virginia Dare Memorial Bridge, the newer of the two bridges that connected Roanoke Island with the mainland. The further out over the water he drove, the worse the winds buffeted the Jeep. The rain made it almost impossible to see the lines painted on the pavement. What was the lyrics of that old Michael Stanley Band song? "Thank God for the man who put the white lines on the highway." Well, that didn't matter now. Edward did his best to drive in a straight line, thankful there was no other traffic on the bridge at the moment.

He finally got back onto actual land and onto Roanoke Island, passing the Outer Banks Visitor's Bureau on his right as he kept the Jeep moving east on Route 64. Edward passed the CVS drugstore at the junction of Manteo and Wanchese. Two towns named for Indians that were part of Sir Walter Raleigh's "Lost Colony." The town of Wanchese sat on the southern part of the island; Manteo on the north. Next Edward saw the fishing boats tied up to their moorings at Pirate's Cove Marina. Edward knew in this blow it was unlikely any of the boats would be out trying to get across the bar through Oregon Inlet. The boats, he could make out in the hard rain, mist and wind, were bobbing up and down with each swell like a fishing bobber on a lake. Edward then crested the Washington Baum Bridge taking him high over Roanoke Sound. The current version of the bridge being completed in 1994 replacing the old draw bridge. Generally speaking, the waters of the sound were typically peaceful and flat. Smooth as glass usually. But this day was different. The Roanoke Sound had swells that appeared to be 3 to 4 feet high! Though it was extremely hard to gauge the height in these conditions, way up on top of the bridge.

The winds were blowing harder now as Edward drove further on the Manteo - Nags Head Causeway and got closer and closer to the Atlantic Ocean. The waters of the sound were crashing and breaching the northern part of the road as the winds were howling from the northeast pushing the water onto the causeway. Edward would not be surprised to find that the Whalebone Quality Plus gas station, to the west of the Sugar Creek Seafood restaurant, under water come the next day if this storm persisted as she has been. Arriving at Whalebone Junction, Edward decided to take South Virginia Dare Trail, commonly just called the Beach Road, rather than hopping onto the "Bypass" where the speed limit was higher. As it was, this weather was keeping vehicle speeds down anyway.

As Edward continued down the Beach Road, he passed Jeannette's Pier, originally built in 1939, only to be rebuilt following Hurricane Isabel's fury in

2003. The Flags lining the pier appearing to be "at attention" as they stood straight out from the continuous northeast wind. Not ever a flutter to them, just pulled taunt from the blow.

Further down the road, the rain water puddled on the road in the spot it usually does; in front of the OBX Toy Rentals building at the corner of East Gray Eagle Street, opposite the beach access. As he continued further to the north, Edward took note of some debris blowing in the parking lot of the Windjammer Condominiums, the World War II looking barracks built on stilts on the oceanfront near milepost 15. One of the buildings of the timeshare community looking bald with its missing shingles.

The rain was coming down in sheets, harder than any point of the drive. Edward, once reaching Dare County, switched the car radio off the Tune-In app and listened directly now to Ocean 105. Chris Stephens, who had taken over for Uncle Danny Daniels about a year ago was now the jock on the air. He had an updated forecast, but it had the same old news. Heavy winds and rain all coming from the northeast. The expected tide at Oregon Inlet at 2:11 had come in about an hour ago and it was wreaking havoc on beach-fronts up and down the Dare County beaches. A few houses that had their sand dune washed away during this storm would now be at the mercy of the boiling waters of the Atlantic, as each wave moved higher and higher, and closer and closer to the structure. Not knowing what he would find when he got home, Edward pushed further. Only a couple of more miles till he reached his ocean front home in Nags Head.

Finally, after passing St. Andrew's By-the-Sea Episcopal Church, Kitty Hawk Kites and Edward's favorite barbecue place, Sooey's BBQ and Rib Shack, he arrived at his home, a few blocks north of the Nags Head Fishing pier, across from The Lucky 12 Tavern. The house was built in the last century by one of Edward's great- great or great-great-great grandfathers, he couldn't remember which now. It was built as a summer house that, as it turned out, was hardly ever used. It was just handed down from generation to generation. Edward was ultimately the first real full time resident of the house. The house itself was a smaller one with a much larger one behind it. The dune behind both houses was even larger still, protecting both structures from many a storm and hurricane. The dune itself measuring approximately 20 feet high.

The cement driveway in the front of Edward's house was wide and lined on both sides with crushed shells and a decorative piling and rope. Edward was happy with his little cedar sided, two bedroom, two bathroom house. It was small, only about 975 square feet or so, but it suited his needs just fine. There was no garage to protect the Jeep from the elements so Edward parked on the driveway in front of the house. The much larger house to the rear was owned by an older couple who lived most of the year in South Florida. They had no kids or any other family, so they almost never visited. Preferring instead to stay home in the "Sunshine State." When they did leave South Florida, it was usually on a cruise ship, sailing around the Caribbean. On one of their rare visits about 7 years ago, they entrusted Edward with a key to their house and asked him to watch over their property. Edward was glad to do it, and in return they encouraged Edward to use the larger house whenever he might have guests come into the area. While Edward never did take them up on their generous offer, he did quite often make use of their deck overlooking the ocean while having his coffee in the morning or when enjoying a beer at the end of a productive day.

Edward used the door on the south side of his house, the one protected from the northeast winds and rain. He got inside and switched on the light. There was a very definite chill in the air and Edward, for a split second thought about turning on the heat, but then decided against it. He'd rather wear a hoodie and sweat pants than pay the extra money for the warmth. The luggage in the Jeep would have to wait, he thought, as he stripped off his wet clothes and threw them into the laundry basket in the utility room next to the stacked washer and dryer. He went into his bedroom and pulled on some warm, dry clothes out of his dresser and closet. Edward then went into the kitchen to turn on the Keurig. While the coffee maker was warming up, so was Edward as he went around the house to open the blinds he had closed before rushing out to Bath, just days prior to his father's passing. The sun, barely filtering through the black storm clouds offered very little light as it turned out, but at least it wasn't black as pitch in the house anymore either. The coffee maker was now sufficiently warmed up and Edward dropped in a pod of Cafe Bustelo into it and hit the brew button. The Keurig came to life as it spit hot, black coffee into the cup below.....

Chapter 10

Edward took his steaming cup of hot, black coffee and sat at his desk in his small office. The office is actually the second bedroom with a futon in it for any guests that may stay over. He pulled out the pad of paper from beneath his stack of notebooks and journals that he kept on each end of the desk and scratched out a "to do list."

Number 1 on that list was checking in with Char concerning the research that she might have pulled together for him. Number 2 was calling Katie at the Old Country Kitchen back in Bath to see if Capt'n Petey had been seen or heard from. The rest of the list were more mundane things that needed to be done following his absence. Things like laundry and picking up groceries.

With the list completed and the coffee from his cup drained, Edward was about to pick up the phone to call Char, but decided instead to make another cup of coffee first. With that cup in hand, he picked up the phone and dialed the number to the office.

"Milepost 11 Publishing. This is Billy…."

Kind of surprised that it was Billy answering the office phone and not Char, Edward paused a moment before answering, "Hey Billy, it's Edward. Where's Char?"

"Oh, hey boss. She's up in the prep room pulling together some of that research you asked for." The prep room was in the upper level of the office space that the magazine rented on Baltic Street, behind what used to be the Rear View Mirror Car Museum. It's where Edward, Billy and Char would put the magazine together every month. "You want me to go grab her?"

“No, no, no. Don’t interrupt her.” Edward replied. Just let her know I just made it back into town a few minutes ago and I plan to be in the office tomorrow.” Glancing at his watch, Edward noticed it was now after 4pm. “In fact, the weather is kind of nasty Billy. Why don’t you and Char go ahead and take off for the day. We’ll get together first thing tomorrow morning.”

“Kind of nasty?” Billy replied. “Boss its been like this since yesterday. Likely to continue for a couple, three more days from what I hear. But roger that. We’ll lock her down for the night and see you in the AM.”

With that Edward clicked off the line and crossed item one off his list. Taking another sip of his coffee, he opened up his laptop and did a Google search for the Old Country Kitchen phone number in Bath. He knew that it was only this morning that he left Katie his card with instructions to call if anyone heard from Capt’n Petey, and he trusted that she would, but with the weather being the way it was, Edward was concerned about the old captain. As far as Edward knew, Capt’n Petey was the only person that held the answers to the questions that still plagued Edward, and he still had more questions to ask him.

Edward dialed the number and waited. One ring. Two rings. Three rings. Edward wondered how many rings he should give it before hanging up and trying again later. Now four, five and six rings. Were they closed because the weather was so bad or were they just busy? Seven rings, eight, nine, ten rings and finally Edward hung up. He wasn’t able to cross item two off his list or to satisfy his curiosity about the old sea captain. Vowing to try again that night, Edward now turned his attention to the mundane items. First he’ll throw in a load of laundry. While that was washing, he’d run to the grocery store for some supplies.

Donning a rain slicker and a dry pair of flip flops, Edward exited his house through the door on the south side again to avoid a direct blast of wind and rain. He got into the Jeep, fired up the engine and made his way to the Fresh Market at the Outer Banks Mall.

Edward had a habit of trying to do all of his grocery shopping around the perimeter of the store. He read once that is where all the healthy food is located. The middle aisles all contained the pre-packaged, sodium and preservative filled foods that added inches to his waistline. He was thankful, however, that the beer was located along the perimeter. That means he was able to buy it. In addition to the fresh fruits, vegetables, chicken and fish; he picked up a 12 pack of The Lost Colony Brewery's Kitty Hawk Blonde Ale. It was in the beer aisle that Edward also ran into his buddy Greg Pants, the morning radio jock from the rock station in town.

"Dude, sorry to hear about your old man." Greg said to Edward as he slapped him on the back. "I didn't know until after you had left town. You cool?"

"Yeah, thanks G." Edward replied. It seemed everyone in town just called Greg, G. "Yeah, I'm good. How about you? Heard that the station might be up for sale."

"Naw, man. That's just jive that some negative people are spreading. We're solid. No one is sellin'. Ain't no one buyin' neither."

"That's good" Edward said. "Wouldn't want my buddy to be out of a gig. Probably because he'd come crawling to me looking for a job."

"Dude, you trippin'. You own a magazine. What I know about writin' and stuff?"

"Reckon you got me there G. So, I've been out of the loop, being out of town and all. When is this weather going to finally break. I'm guessing your news staff is staying on top of it all."

“Don’t think its gonna happen this week dude. It looks like its gonna be blowin’ and blowin’ and rainin’ and rainin’ for the next several days. This spring tide thing ain’t helpin’ either. Lots of houses might be at risk. Maybe some hotels too.”

“Wow....that bad, huh?”

“Yeah dude. It’s a big one.”

“Well, stay dry and stay safe G.” Edward responded. And I hope all that radio station talk being sold is all that; just talk.”

The two men bumped fists as Edward made his way to the check out line. $88.39 later, he was running back through the wind and the rain with 5 bags of groceries to his Jeep. Instead of heading for home, at the last minute Edward decided to drop by the office to see if Char had left the research material for him. He figured he could at least read it over tonight.

Edward waited at the stop light to turn left out of the Outer Banks Mall parking lot and onto the Bypass. Cars, whizzing past splashing water onto each other from all the puddles. While Edward waited at the light, he even saw a pedestrian, waiting to cross the street get blasted by standing water from a car. The pedestrian couldn’t get any wetter, Edward thought, but still....

Finally the light changed to green. Edward put the Jeep into first gear from neutral and waited for the pedestrian to cross before pulling out onto the road. For a split second he thought about asking the lone walker if they needed a ride, but in this day and age he decided against it, still feeling guilty though as he made the turn. A few minutes later Edward pulled the Jeep into the parking lot of Milepost 11 Publishing.

The office for the publishing company was an old summer house that was converted into office space. At first, the publishing company only rented the space on the first floor, but as the years went by and the magazine became more popular and therefore more profitable, Edward leased the entire building/house. In fact, he was now in negotiations with the owner to buy it outright.

The building was dark. Edward was glad that Billy and Char took him up on his offer to leave early. He ran from the Jeep to the front door. Unfortunately the door faced the northeast and it was a struggle to pull open the screen against the oncoming wind. Once opened, it was a struggle to get the wooden door shut again behind him while keeping out as much of the rain as possible.

The original summer house was set up on a typical vacation reverse floor plan. The bedrooms were located on the lower floor while the kitchen and living space was located on the upper level. Now, the prep room was upstairs, the individual offices were downstairs. Edward reached for the light switch located to the right of the door. He flipped it up and the office space came to life. He walked past Char's desk in the center of the hallway and entered the first room on the right. That was his office. Off that was a "Jack and Jill" bathroom that connected to a second office where Billy did most of his work. Across the hall would have been a third bedroom, but now housed the printer, the copier, the fax machine, and various office supplies.

Edward's office was a bit cluttered, much like his brain. Things stacked here. Things stacked there. However, in a pinch he was able to locate exactly what he was looking for in those stacks. It may not have been the perfect filing system, but it seemed to work well enough for Edward. There was a credenza directly behind his desk, and on it standing as the centerpieces were two things. A picture of his mother and father on the day Edward was born, and a framed map of his hometown of Bath, North Carolina. It was given to him by his father the day Edward left for college at Chapel Hill as a way of reminding him where his roots are located.

Edward hit the power switch on the Keurig that he kept on a small table in his office. While waiting for the machine to warm up he sat down in his black leather desk chair and looked at the picture of his mother and father and then the framed map. His thoughts drifted to the conversation he first had with Capt'n Petey about this not being the time for the old captain to let Edward in on the conversation between him and his father. He wondered why Capt'n Petey disappeared. He wondered where he went. Edward also wondered about the Teach's Light phenomenon and what all that meant. He wondered how men and women in the 21st century are able to just brush off any real answer to the light. Even his friend Wes Walker, who never believed in anything, could not offer up any plausible explanation.

Just then a crash of an outside tree limb startled Edward out of his thoughts. He went over to the window to find a branch from the old Atlantic White Cedar on the neighboring property had crashed onto the roof of that structure. Not seemingly to have caused any real damage, Edward went back to the coffee maker and dropped a coffee pod into it and hit "brew." Despite his instruction to Char to always buy Cafe Bustelo, instead she would always buy whatever happened to be on sale. This week is apparently Folger's Black Silk.

Once done brewing, Edward grabbed his coffee and sat back down at his desk. On it, he found the story that Billy had written about the Theater of Dare and it's upcoming season. Billy had done a good job on it, Edward thought. He covered every aspect of the story he himself would have covered. Also in the folder was a couple of new contracts for advertising. One for Josephine's Sicilian Kitchen in Kitty Hawk. Another for Stripers Bar & Grille in Manteo. Setting that file back down, Edward, thought to himself that Billy was working out just fine, and he should probably let him know that tomorrow when he sees him. Next Edward picked up the file that Char had left for him. The research on Blackbeard. He opened it and found approximately 20 - 25 pages in it. Knowing he had groceries in the car that needed to be refrigerated, Edward finished the last of the coffee, tucked the folder inside his rain slicker and made his way back out into the mess Mother Nature was hellbent on continuing.

Once back in the Jeep, Edward turned right out of the parking lot onto Baltic Street, made his way past the abandoned car museum and out to the Beach Road, where he turned right again, for the mile drive home. Most days Edward would either walk or bicycle to work, it was that close. That likely wasn't going to happen in the next several days. The Beach Road now looked more like a river than a road. Water was streaming down it from north to south. If there is much more of this, Edward might start worrying about flooding at his house.

Edward got home and put all the groceries away and moved the wet clothes from the washer to the dryer. Realizing that he hadn't eaten since breakfast, he threw together a large salad with berries and an avocado sliced on top, and finished it off with a coconut-mango dressing. He then sat down with a Lost Colony Blonde Ale and began to read Char's file.

The file contained two accounts of Teach's Light. One from Dr. T. P. Bonner, son of Joseph Bonner (the man who built the Bonner House and for whom Bonner's Point is named). The very place where Edward himself experienced the phenomenon. Dr. Bonner's tale was eerily similar to Edward's:

There have been seen many strange phenomena at the mouth of Bath Creek, incomprehensible to all who have witnessed it. I, myself, am not superstitious. I have seen the smoke of battle for four years, and my limbs bear an eternal witness to the fact; and am not frightened at a myth; but I must admit that a feeling of awe possessed me, as with my father and a dozen other men, of reputable reputation, I have stood on my father's piazza during a violent storm, when the river and the creek was a mass of foam, and the spume was seathed like a snow storm.

A ball of fire as large or larger than a man's head, sailed back and forth from Plum Point (location of Teach's home) to Archbell Point all that night without any deviation from a direct line, while the wind was blowing at the rate of 40 miles an hour. No phosphorescent or jelly mass could have withstood the gale without being swept out of existence. There are men living today who will substantiate all I write. This occurred during every violent storm.

The other account came from the Reverend J. W. Sneeden, a former pastor of the Bath Methodist Church. No one doubted what this man of the cloth said when he told his story publicly.

Also within the pages of the file were accounts of the “Light” in other locations other than just in the town of Bath. There have been sightings by local fishermen on Ocracoke Island, in the very channel where Blackbeard was killed, right here on the Outer Banks. The legend there says that Blackbeard is searching for his missing head so his friends will be able to recognize him.

All very interesting reading of course, but nothing that pointed to any scientific reasoning behind the light. Edward was no closer to an answer than when he first started his quest.

Edward set those pages off to the side. He next concentrated on the pages of research devoted to Blackbeard's wife. There are reports that the pirate captain had up to 14 wives and 13 children. There was even a report that Blackbeard tried to court Governor Eden's daughter (the then governor of North Carolina), but was rebuffed because she was already engaged to another man. Apparently Char did some further research and found that Governor Eden never even had a daughter, although he did have a step-daughter named Penelope. Proving that folklore just can't be trusted as fact.

It seems that of the apparent 14 wives that Blackbeard was to have taken, only Mary Ormond is mentioned as being his legal wife. The others were likely just women Blackbeard carried on with at various ports. Mary was the daughter of a plantation owner from Bath. It was Governor Eden, who in 1718, performed the actual wedding ceremony. Mary was only 16 years old at the time. The report goes on to say that a few months following the marriage, the call of the sea was too strong for Blackbeard to ignore any longer, and with Mary pregnant with his child, he left Bath forever only to die a few months later on November 22.

Following the departure of Blackbeard from Bath, almost nothing was again reported about Mary Ormond except that she gave birth to a baby boy after Blackbeard was already dead. A boy she named Edward Teach Jr

Edward set this research aside and was lost in his thoughts when a loud buzz from the dryer indicated his clothes were dry. It startled him back to reality.

Edward got up from his desk, taking his dirty dinner plate and fork with him and set them in the sink. He threw away his now empty Lost Colony Blonde Ale bottle and went to grab his clothes from the dryer to fold them and to put them away.

A few minutes later, Edward was back at his desk to continue his reading, but not before grabbing another Lost Colony Blonde. He sat back down in his chair. With the house quiet, he could hear the storm still raging outside. The wind was howling and the rain was pelting the north side windows of the house, coming down in an obvious slant. Before picking up the next page of research he said out loud: “Alexa, what's the weather”

The Amazon Echo perched on the right corner of his desk came to life and said:

“Currently in Nags Head it's 51 degrees with heavy rain. Look for much of the same tonight and into tomorrow. The low tonight will be 46 with a gale warning posted.”

Edward chuckled as he said to himself, “why did I even expect it to be better?”

Edward took a sip out of his Blonde Ale and picked up the next set of pages of research. The last thing he had asked Char to look into was the derivation of Blackbeard's surname: Teach.

The report showed that there is some argument as to what Blackbeard's real name was. All reports agree that his first name is Edward, although he was often referred to as Ned. But those same reports differ when it comes to the last name. Some say it's Teach. Others say its Thatch. There are even several different spellings that have been uncovered: Thatch, Thack, Theach, Thatche, Thache. There was even one account that the infamous pirate's last name was Drummond. But supporting evidence of this was never uncovered and it was quickly dismissed.

Edward set his reading material down, as this was getting too close to home now. His own name, and that of his father, was eerily close to that of the pirate. Edward Drummond Thatcher. Edward had no idea what any of it meant. He had questions that needed to be answered, and as far as he knew, only one person was in a position to answer those questions. And for the moment anyway, that person was missing.

Edward checked the clock. It was nearing 8:30 pm. He was sure the Old Country Kitchen in Bath would be closed by now, but he called the number nonetheless. Just in case someone may still be there.

One ring. Two rings. Three rings. Edward resolved to give it a few more seconds just in case. Four, five, six rings. No answer. Same as earlier today. Edward clicked the cell phone off. A little aggravated, he jotted a note to himself to try again first thing in the morning.

Edward picked up the last page of research compiled by his secretary. It simply said that the only treasure that had ever been recovered as a result of Blackbeard's piracy was taken by what had been presumed to be wreckage of the Queen Anne's Revenge, Blackbeard's ship. That discovery came in 1996 and as recently as a few years ago, more than 250,000 artifacts had been recovered. Most of it on display at the North Carolina Maritime Museum.

Edward put all the research back into its folder and set it on the corner of his desk. He sat there a good long while trying to absorb all that he read. Trying to put it all into some sort of perspective. It seemed the longer he sat there, the more questions came to the surface. What was it his father had been trying to tell him all these years? What is it exactly that Capt'n Petey knows, but won't say? Where is Capt'n Petey? Why all the similarities surrounding his name with that of Blackbeard? What is "Teach's Light" exactly?

The storm was still raging outside. Edward knew that sooner or later that he was going to have to bring in his luggage from the Jeep. It wasn't going to get any calmer or drier anytime soon. And since Edward wasn't one to procrastinate, he put on the rain slicker and in bare feet ran out to empty the car.

After two quick trips Edward had everything back in the house. The real reason he ran out into the weather was because he wanted to do some additional reading. In his suitcase, Edward had carefully wrapped in his underwear the very brittle copy of "*Pyrates and Buccaneers of the Carolinas.*" He opened the book to where he left off and started reading. It was almost an hour later when he had completed reading about Bath's most infamous son and still had no additional answers. Carefully, Edward closed the book and put it on top of Char's file. The clock now indicating that it was 11 pm, Edward thought it best to get some sleep and start fresh in the morning. Hopefully, the storm would taper off while he dreamt.

Chapter 11

Edward flopped onto his bed. He was one of those people that didn't like to sleep. Unnecessary waste of time he would often say. But he knew that if he didn't get at least his 6 hours he was worthless the next day.

Edward grabbed the tv remote from the nightstand on his right. He hit the power button and dialed it over to the Weather Channel. He was shocked to find they were broadcasting just up the road from Jennette's Pier, on the south end of Nags Head. Apparently there is a slow enough weather pattern that they actually brought someone in to cover a gale. True, it was a gale on a spring tide, but still...

The last thing Edward remembered was the voice of Jim Cantore saying "reporting LIVE from Nags Head." He woke up the next morning without benefit of an alarm clock, which was his norm. Edward was one of those rare people. The kind of person that meets each day with zeal and a passion for the upcoming day. He loved what he did as a matter of his life's work and he felt grateful to be able to do it.

Edward stood up, stretched and went to the window. He didn't need to look outside however. He was able to hear the storm still raging. Edward lifted the blind at the back of the house looking eastward towards the Atlantic. He could not see the water due to the large house and even larger dune behind him, but what he did see was enough. Rain was pelting the ground which was already past its saturation point. The wind still howling out of the northeast. No doubt about it, it was going to be a mess today.

Edward went into the bathroom and got his morning routine out of the way. Shave, shower and brush his teeth. He then made his way back downstairs to make some coffee and to try calling the Old Country Kitchen.

Coffee in hand, Edward settled back into his chair at his desk and dialed the restaurant's number, holding his breath that he would get an answer this time.....

One ring. Two rings....."Old County Kitchen. This is Hunter."

"Oh, hey Hunter. Um, my name is Edward. I had breakfast there a few days ago with Capt'n Petey...."

"Yeah. You're the western omelet and ham guy..."

"Uh, yeah. I think I did have that. How do you remember that?"

"If somebody gives me way more than the standard 20% tip I have a tendency to remember them," Hunter replied. "What can I do for you, um, Edward?"

"Well, I was hoping to speak with your sister Katie. Is she around?"

"I'm sorry Edward. She's not. We closed early yesterday due to the storm blowing out power to the area and she's at home taking care of things there. But she did mention that you might call."

"I hope everything is ok," Edward said.

"Yeah, fine. Everything's fine. But she wanted me to tell you, in case you called, that no one has seen or heard from Capt'n Petey yet. In fact she mentioned if she doesn't hear from him by the end of the week, she was going to call Chief Haney to see about making out a missing person report."

"Ok, thanks for the information Hunter. Let me ask you, is it normal for Capt'n Petey to just disappear like this? I mean, not to be seen or heard from for days?"

"Well Edward" Hunter said, pausing briefly to collect his thoughts, "I would say it was abnormal. We would often go without seeing him for a while, but I will say, its never been in weather like this. Usually when the weather is blowing this hard it seems that he spends most of his days and nights here killing time."

"Hmmm," was all Edward could muster as a response. "Well, Ok Hunter. You guys have my number. If there's anything I can do to help, please let me know. And if you hear or see the old capt'n please give me a call."

"Will do," Hunter replied, as both men clicked off the call.

Edward set his phone down on the desk and absentmindedly finished the rest of his coffee. Glancing at the clock, he noticed it to be only 8:20 am. Might as well have another cup of coffee before heading in. At least here he could enjoy a good cup of Cafe Bustelo.

Coffee finished and knowing that Char and Billy likely wouldn't be in for another 30 minutes or so, Edward grabbed his rain slicker and ran out to the Jeep. He thought it would be nice that when they got there they would have some hot coffee and pastry waiting for them so he made a trip to the Front Porch Cafe on his way to the office.

It seemed impossible, but the rain was coming down even harder now. The wind even stronger. Edward turned right out of his driveway. It seemed like he was a salmon on a spawn run, going upriver, even in the 4 wheel drive Jeep. The water was rushing past his wheels on its Mother Nature created river bed called the Beach Road. Even harder and faster than it had been the previous day. He tuned left onto East Abalone Street and another left into the parking lot of the Front Porch Cafe. Few cars were parked in the lot, the storm seemingly keeping the usual morning crowd away. Edward, bracing himself yet again from the wind and the rain, opened the driver's side door of the Jeep and raced for the front door of the cafe.

Once inside, it occurred to Edward that Char had the same idea, as she was already at the counter ordering for her, Edward and Billy.

“Hey you!” Edward called out to Char.

“Oh hey boss. Figured we could all use a little pick me up from this dismal, gray weather.” Char replied. It was times like this that she didn’t particularly care for living on the Outer Banks. But she figured it was much better than the snow storms of Cleveland that she moved away from some dozen years ago.

“I should have figured you had Billy and me covered this morning. You always seem to take care of us like we were your kids or something.”

“Or something.” Char laughed.

Edward knew it would be a futile exercise to try to get Char to take any money for the coffee and food, so he didn’t try. Never in all the years has she ever taken a penny as reimbursement for doing a good deed. Not many altruistic people like this left in the world, and Edward was darn glad to have her.

“Here, at least let me carry this stuff out to my Jeep and into the office. That way you can stay dry under your umbrella.”

“Umbrella? In this wind? But I’ll take you up on your offer of taking these things back to work. At least my hands will be free and I can make it to and from my car quicker.”

“You got it. See you in a few minutes.” Edward said. “And, oh, by the way, thanks again for this.”

“No worries Chief. See you in a few.”

Char went out into the elements, hopped into her car and drove through the rain and the wind to the office of Milepost 11 Publishing.

Edward gathered up some creamers and sugar for the coffees. He took his black, but the others didn't. He then ran out of the cafe and jumped into his Jeep. He drove back down East Abalone Street to Wrightsville Avenue where he took a right. From there he pointed his Jeep to East Baltic Street where he took another right hand turn and into the parking lot of his magazine company.

Char was already inside, of course, getting things ready for the day. She checked the messages from last night, which there were none. She was now checking the company's email as Edward walked through the door. With a quizzical look on her face she said, "Hey boss. Got kind of weird email here."

"Really?" Edward asked.

"Well I think so…." Char continued, "Can't really tell if it's spam or not."

Edward now curious replied "What makes you think it's spam?"

"Well, it's from Ancestry.com. It says they have information you were looking for."

A few weeks ago, when first getting the bad news about his father's pancreatic cancer, sitting outside the ICU while doctors and nurses worked on keeping Edward Sr. as comfortable as possible, Edward started completing the forms for Ancestry.com. It had come at a weak moment when Edward the son realized that his father wasn't going to be able to provide the family history due to his illness. He wasn't talking much at that point. And what he was saying wasn't making a whole lot of sense.

Having almost forgotten about it, Edward told Char to go ahead and forward it to his personal email account.

After distributing the coffee and breakfast food that Char had picked out for the three, and giving some words of praise to Billy for a job well done on his latest article and ad sales, Edward went into his office, shut the door and opened his personal email account.

“What is that about?” Billy asked Char. “He never closes his door.”

“Yeah, that is rare indeed. But we must remember he just lost his dad and I’m sure he is feeling pretty poorly right now. And I’m sure this weather isn’t helping his mood any. I know it’s not helping mine. Let’s just give him space today. Let him work some things out.”

“Guess you’re right Char. I hope he’s ok.”

“Yeah. Me too,” Char replied. “Hey nice job landing Josephine's and Stripers. I’m sure those accounts will go a long way in helping Edward with his mood.”

“Yeah. Maybe.” Billy replied, as he went back into his office to make some calls. Billy wanted to keep himself abreast of this Nor’easter. It’s the first one he had ever experienced.

Char also went back to work. She pulled out the copy she made for herself of all the Blackbeard research. She wanted to see what more she could contribute to it. There’s more to Edward’s mood than just the weather and his father she thought, as she turned her attention to her computer screen.

Chapter 12

In his office, Edward too had his attention focused on the computer screen in front of him. Specifically on the email from Ancestry.com. The email contained what the website calls "hints." It's a little green leaf on the upper right side that you click on. It gives you some possible family members based on the information provided them on your initial paperwork. You either accept them or ignore them, based on how you feel about the match. There were some "hints" of various cousins. First cousins, once, twice, thrice removed. Edward moved quickly past those. He wasn't necessarily interested in those folks. There was one "hint" however that caught Edward's immediate attention. Something he had never heard of prior to now. Apparently Edward's father, Edward Drummond Thatcher Senior, had a brother that was given away for adoption when only a couple of days old. No reason as to why he was given up. And the only name he could find for this baby were just the initials P.E. Thatcher.

Not much to go one, Edward thought. But interesting nonetheless. Could this person hold the key to the answers? Would this person even know the answers? Having been given up for adoption, seemingly immediately after being born it seemed unlikely. The more Edward dug into his family, the more questions he gets. Hardly any answers at all.

Edward opened another tab on his computer. He opened the website for Beaufort County, North Carolina, the county in which Bath is a part. He found the phone number for the County Register of Deeds. Edward figured this was a good a place to start as any. He wanted to see if he could track down the birth certificate of a P. E. Thatcher.

After being kept on hold for nearly 20 minutes. Nineteen minutes and 47 seconds to be exact, Edward had no real answer. But he did have a birth date. P. E. Thatcher was born September 28, 1942. That was two years before Edward Sr. was born. Why he had been given up was still a mystery. Perhaps P. E. was born to a single mother? Quite the stigma in the early 1940's. Was the father off at war and the boy was born illegitimately to a lonely "war widow"? All speculations at best. Maybe the answer as to why the baby was given up wasn't even that important. What seemed more important at the moment was finding the last living link Edward Jr. had to his father.

Thoughts of hiring a private investigator came to mind. A Jim Rockford type, Edward thought. Someone who for only "$200 a day plus expenses" could help locate P.E. That notion only lasted a few fleeting moments. Wasn't he after all, the owner of a magazine? Couldn't he just do the research himself? He, in what seemed to be another lifetime, was once an investigative reporter…

Edward was startled back into reality with the ringing of his cell phone. It was a number he knew. It was the Old Country Kitchen. Hoping for good news, but bracing for bad, Edward answered the phone apprehensively.

Hello, this is Edward."

"Oh, hi Edward. This is Katie from the Old Country Kitchen."

"Hey Katie." Edward replied. "Everything ok? You hear from Petey?"

"No sir, sadly I haven't." Katie, paused before continuing. "I know you spoke to Hunter this morning, but I wanted to call too, to let you know that I was thinking of talking to Chief Haney."

"Yes Hunter mentioned that."

“Yes, I know he did. But I wanted to ask your opinion. I was going to wait till the end of the week to do it......but I don’t know....”

“Don’t know what?” Edward asked.

“Well, should I not wait? Should I talk to the chief sooner?”

Edward paused for a moment, not knowing how to guide the young girl who seemed very obviously concerned. Finally he replied, “From what Hunter has told me, Petey would often wait out storms at the restaurant, so it was unlike him to be gone now. Would you agree with Hunter on that?”

“Yeah. That’s what I mean.” Katie gulped back what seemed like a small sob before continuing on, “If the weather was good, I wouldn’t be concerned not seeing him this long, but since the weather is bad....”

Not giving Katie a chance to finish her sentence, Edward blurted out, “Tell you what Katie, how ‘bout I call the chief? See if maybe I can have the police do some poking around. Maybe they’ll know where he usually hangs out.”

“Would you Edward? That would be great!”

“Sure Katie. I’ll call him this morning.”

“Thanks Edward! I know it’s probably nothing. But still, it could be something.”

“Well, let’s hope for the best. I’ll call you once I hear something.”

“Thanks Edward. I really appreciate it!”

With that, both Edward and Katie clicked off their call.

Edward stood and stretched. His coffee from the Front Porch Cafe now cold, so he went into the Jack and Jill bathroom to empty the cup into the sink. He went over to the Keurig and switched it on to warm up. After a few seconds he dropped in a Folger Black Silk coffee pod and hit “brew.” While the coffee was trickling into his cup Edward went over to the window and lifted the blind. Still raining hard. Still blowing hard. And so dark it almost looked like it was nearly night, despite the fact that it was only 10:38 am.

Once the coffee was ready, he grabbed his cup and went back into the hallway where Char was at her desk.

“Everything ok boss?”

“Yeah. Fine. Just working on a bit of a mystery.” Edward replied.

“Anything having to do with that email?”

Edward moved over to the small office couch tucked next to the front door and sat down heavily into it. He took a long sip of his fresh coffee and replied, “well, I guess 2 mysteries. The one from the email and one having to do with an old sea captain back home.”

Char, never having heard Edward refer to Bath as “back home” must have been visibly surprised causing Edward to react with, “Yeah, I know. This is home. Has been for a long time now. Just have a lot on my mind right now. Sorry.”

“No worries boss.” She answered back.

Just then the two were joined by Billy who had emerged from his office. “Hey guys, the National Weather says that we are in a full blown Nor'easter!” He exclaimed.

Edward and Char looked at each other for a split second and then both busted out laughing.

"What? What?!?!" Billy wanted to know. "What's so funny?"

Edward stood back up, walked over to Billy and put his arm around him. "Char, why don't you tell our young, Midwestern colleague here what's so funny."

Trying to compose herself before speaking, Char stood up and also put her arm around Billy. "Well Billy, all you had to do is ask either Edward or me....or anyone here on the Outer Banks for that matter. Any one of us could have told you that this was a Nor'easter. You didn't really need to bother the National Weather Service for that."

Feeling a little silly at this point, all Billy could muster was a "Oh, sorry. I never saw one of these back in Ohio."

"That's ok boy" Edward replied. "Just hate to see what will happen when you experience your first hurricane!"

With that, Billy's face turned white as a sheet.

"Ok, that's enough boss! Don't scare this poor boy silly!" Char jumped in trying to protect Billy.

"Just funnin' ya son." Edward said with a smirk on his face. "You'll do just fine when a hurrykin' comes a callin'."

Billy turned to go back to his office and said softly to himself "Hurricane? It gets worse than this?"

Edward also made his way back to his office and once again closed his door....

Chapter 13

Looking through his recent calls on his cellphone, Edward located the non-emergency phone number he used a short time ago to call Chief Haney to report "Teach's Light." He hit dial....Three rings later Edward got an answer.

"Bath Police, Officer Meekins." The officer pronouncing it PO – lease.

"Hi Officer Meekins. My name is Edward Thatcher. Is Chief Haney around?"

"Nah, sir. The chief, he's out on a call right now. Big tree fell acrost the road during the storm. Really made a mess of things. Can't get from one side of town to th'other." Likely he'll be a while. He asked me to stay back and answer the phones in case of an emergency. This an emergency sir?"

"Well, I'm not sure if it is or not officer." Edward responded.

"Well sir, either it is or it is not."

"No I guess not Officer Meekins. At least not yet anyway. Can you have the Chief give me a call when he's able?"

"Reckon I can do that fer ya."

After giving Officer Meekins his phone number, Edward hung up his cell phone.

Noticing that he only had 19% power left on the phone, Edward plugged it in and placed it on the credenza behind his desk. He then flipped on the tv he had sitting on a bookcase on the far side of the room. The television already tuned to The Weather Channel as another report was being broadcast down the street. Edward didn't catch the reporter's name, but did recognize that he was beside Jennette's Pier. Those cement "legs" of the pier making it stand out from all the other piers along the Outer Banks.

The reporter commented on the wind, still strong out of the northeast. He commented on the beach erosion and he said something that Edward hadn't heard before. The reporter was talking about the possibilities of sand escarpments developing due to the high tides and high winds and the constant barrage of waves on the beach. Escarpments, the reporter went on to say, were erosion that form sand ledges or cliffs. There will be "huge drop-offs with these cliffs" so care was needed if out on the beaches during the storm.

A quick Google search taught Edward that in conditions such as the Outer Banks were experiencing, sand escarpments were typically temporary and generally smooth themselves out, once the prevailing south west winds eventually return.

Having never really seen an escarpment, Edward made a mental note to take a stroll out into the storm in the next day or two to see one for himself. He left the tv on about 10 more minutes, not really paying much attention to it, while his thoughts drifted. It was at that point the knock on the door that rocked Edward back to reality.

"Come in," Edward yelled out.

"Hey boss," Char said as she opened the door. "Sorry to bother you, but wanted to see if you needed anything. Billy and I were talking about having a pizza delivered for lunch. Wondered if you wanted in on that."

"Sure, but only under two conditions."

"No, we won't get broccoli on it! I know you hate broccoli." Char replied.

"Ok, three conditions." Edward said laughing. "Yes, no pizza with broccoli, but that should just be a given. Whomever invented putting broccoli on a pizza just ain't right in the head!"

"What's 2 and 3?" Char asked.

"Two is that I pay for it. My treat. And 3, once we're done eating, we get out of here for the day. It's slow. We don't need to put the magazine together for a couple of more days, and this weather is just depressing."

"Well boss, I can speak for Billy on your first point. No broccoli, we'll agree to that. But on 2 and 3......I just don't know. I mean, who wants free pizza and an afternoon off?" Char said with a laugh. "Thanks boss. I'll order it now."

Char walked back out of the office, closing the door behind her, leaving Edward to drift back to the thoughts inside his head.

And drift inside his head he did. He went back to the computer and did a Google search for P.E. Thatcher. He came up with nothing. "Likely a dead end," Edward said to himself. If P.E was adopted, he likely exists under whatever his name is now. Adoption files are typically sealed. It wasn't likely Edward was going to find out anything more on this using conventional methods. It was obvious that Edward was going to have to think outside the box to solve this mystery.

Having already talked to Katie at the diner and having tried reaching out to Chief Haney at the police station, Edward wasn't really sure what else he could do at the moment, so he turned his attention to some of the mundane tasks having to do with the magazine. He edited a couple of the free lance writer pieces that would be included in the current issue. He also wrote some captions for the photos that would be part of the articles. Lastly, he also wrote an intro to Billy's story on the Theatre of Dare. Once those were completed it wasn't too much later that Char announced that the "pizza is here!"

Edward went into the copier room and grabbed paper plates and napkins for the lunch now sitting on Char's desk. Nags Head Pizza Company outdid themselves again. Char ordered the Pesto Chicken pizza with roasted mushrooms, goat cheese and mozzarella. Perfect for the rainy, dreary afternoon.

Char sat at her desk, sharing it with Billy while Edward sat on the couch with his plate sitting on the cushion next to him. For the 20 minutes that it took to polish off the entire pizza, the trio didn't discuss anything work related. Mostly the talk was about the date young Billy had just prior to the storm. The girl lived in Wanchese, the daughter of one of the Wicked Tuna OBX television stars. They had a nice dinner at Sooey's BBQ before heading off to play miniature golf over at Jurassic Putt in Nags Head. Both Char and Edward giving Billy a hard time about being a boring date.

"What? It was a nice night!" Billy exclaimed.

"A nice dull night you mean," Char added.

"Edward. Tell Char that was a perfect respectable evening!" Billy again exclaimed looking for male back up in the argument.

Before giving Edward a chance to weigh in, Char blurted out, "Respectable yes, but let me spell it out for you B-O-R-I-N-G!"

"What's boring to one may not be to another," Billy said.

"Let me ask you Billy," Char continued. "Have you been out since?"

"Well no, we haven't."

"Have you asked her out since?" Char wanted to know.

"Well, yes, but she's been busy."

"Yeah, busy dodging you, I'd expect," Char retorted.

It was at this point that Edward felt the need to interject. “Come on Char. Leave poor old Billy alone. He’s just not a worldly man of the world yet.”

“Thanks....I think.” Billy said not quite knowing if Edward was sticking up for him or mocking him.

“Alright you two. Let’s clean this empty box and napkins up and call it a day. I’ll see you two back here again tomorrow around 9.” Edward said to Char and Billy.

Not content yet to stop picking at Billy, Char replied “Now don’t get too wild tonight son!”

Taking full advantage of Char’s reluctance to always be known as the “mother hen” of the office, due to her advanced age when compared to Billy and Edward, Billy simply answered with a “yes mom.”

Char shot the young reporter a sideways glance as they opened the door and ran through the wind and the rain to their cars to begin their afternoon free from work.

Chapter 14

Edward now back at home, made himself some coffee and sat down in his chair to watch more of The Weather Channel. Nothing had changed in the forecast. Wind from the northeast, more rain, more beach erosion. A few minutes later the in-studio anchor sent it out to the field reporter who was back on the scene next to Jennette's Pier. He was warning residents and visitors once again about the escarpments, particularly the one that was located to his north, near milepost 11.

That perked Edward right up! Milepost 11? That's exactly where he was. Edward drained the rest of the coffee from his cup and prepared to dress for the weather. He put on his rain slicker and some waders he would occasionally use for some inland fishing trips. Edward, again using the door on the south side of the house, went outside and up his driveway to the large house behind his. He figured he'd go there first to scout what he could from the large deck on the back of the house. Bending against the wind, he finally made it to the covered porch, although the porch provided almost no cover at all. The rain was still coming down sideways. From here Edward looked up and down the beach. He couldn't see much. The blowing sand and the rain saw to that. Plus, the large sand dune protecting the house from the now angry, gray waters of the Atlantic still stood taller than Edward.

Carefully Edward stepped down from the porch to climb to the top of the dune. The rain and the sand combined forces to make each step very difficult as he blindly inched his way to the top. Once there, he couldn't believe what he saw! The other side of the dune; the side facing the Atlantic Ocean was a sheer cliff down to the water's edge. But it wasn't just a straight drop. The other side of the dune was concave, and Edward was standing on the lip of the wind and water driven sand cave. Figuring that this might not be the safest place to be, Edward scampered back down the side he climbed up as quickly as he could.

Back on the covered porch, soaked to the bone, Edward's curiosity got the better of him. From what he could tell from the top, the hollowed out area of the dune extended past the big house, toward the vacant rental house to the south. Figuring he couldn't get any wetter, Edward hopped down from the porch and walked with the wind and rain at his back toward the vacant house. This house, from it's back deck, had a wooden walkway that went over top of the sand dune where a gazebo sat above the sand. On the other side of the gazebo was a staircase that would take him down to the beach.

Protected by all that Mother Nature threw at him, Edward was able to climb up to the back deck on the south side of the house. Even though he lived next to this house for a number of years, this was the first time Edward had ever been on this deck. There was a locked gate leading from the deck to the walkway over the dune. Presumably to keep people from trespassing on the property while the house was vacant. Edward, however, hopped over the railing, holding onto the gate itself and inched his way to the other side. Once past it, he swung himself back onto the walkway and made his way down to the gazebo.

From the gazebo, Edward looked to the north. He could barely make out an opening to the sand cave. Deciding to take a closer look, Edward went to the staircase leading down to the beach. Due to the wind and the rain and the surf, the beach below was almost completely washed away. Edward got down to the last step and had to jump down at least four feet to the beach below. How he was going to get back up again, he wasn't quite sure.

Keeping as close to the dune as possible, while at the same time keeping as much distance from the angry surf of the ocean, Edward inched his way north to the entrance of the sand cave. The dune loomed over top of him, nearly 15 feet high. This stretch of beach, normally one of the busiest and most crowded in Nags Head, was now eerily empty. Who in their right mind would be out in this mess, Edward wondered to himself.

With each passing minute the tide got higher and higher. Full blown high tide was due within the next half hour. Edward wouldn't have time dawdle. If he didn't want to risk being caught in a riptide he knew he was going to have to get back up on the safety of the deck soon. His curiosity had gotten the better of him however. He kept walking north and finally stood at the entrance of what looked like an entrance to a cave that burrowed under the dune, running toward his house. The Atlantic, roughed up by Mother Nature and the gravitational pull of the moon lapped angrily around his ankles as he stood there in disbelief. With his back to the ocean, Edward took a small step into the mouth of the cave. There was something in there. He could see it. It was about 20 yards deeper into the cave. He couldn't quite make out what it was, another corridor perhaps.

Suddenly, from out of nowhere, a rogue wave crashed at the entrance of the cave, knocking Edward down to his backside. The cold water of the Atlantic filling his waders. The undertow pulled Edward back out again and onto the beach. Or what was left of the beach at this point. He pulled himself back to his feet and figuring that discretion was the better part of valor, retraced his steps back to the staircase from where he originally jumped down onto the beach.

Edward arrived back at the staircase. The bottom rung, being a full four feet above his head. He jumped to grab a hold of the bottom step. He missed by nearly 2 feet. The wet sand not exactly creating a solid platform from which to jump. Edward jumped again. Again, he missed by at least half the distance. Hoping that "three times is the charm". Edward jumped and he missed again. It turned out that it was "three strikes and he was out." On the third attempt Edward came crashing down into a clump as another wave washed over him.

The tide was getting higher now. No time to be stranded on an already quickly eroding beach in the middle of a gale. Edward started walking down the beach toward the south, looking for a place to get off the beach. Finally after 10 minutes he was able to scamper back up to the Beach Road and off the beach at the Nags Head Fishing Pier. He saw the red “No Swimming” flags flying there and said to himself, “yeah, no kidding.”

Finding himself a quarter of a mile from his house, Edward slogged back home as the wind and the rain hit him head on.

Chapter 15

Finally back home, Edward peeled off the rain slicker and waders in his outdoor shower rather than taking them into the house. He was already wet anyway, taking the protective clothing off outside didn't matter to the clothes underneath them. At least this way he didn't have to drag those wet items through the house. Once down to his shorts and t-shirt, Edward ran for the warmth and dryness of his home.

Edward had left his cell phone at home when he went exploring. He didn't want it to get wet out in the elements. As he stood at the doorway pulling off his wet clothes he heard it ringing in his office. But by the time he was free of the wet clothing and started sprinting for it, it had stopped ringing.

As the final ring had ended, Edward picked it up from his desk. He noticed 1 voice mail and 6 missed calls, all from the same number. All in the approximate hour he was outside. He recognized the number immediately. It was the non-emergency number from the Bath, North Carolina Police Department. Edward put the voice mail on speaker and hit "play."

"Hi Mr Thatcher" the message began.

"Chief Haney here from Bath. A couple of things have come up here in town that both directly and indirectly affect you. One of which I will need a written statement or written complaint from you. Unfortunately I will need you to make a return trip to town. Can you call me as quickly as you can please?"

Still standing naked and wet in his office, Edward thought that whatever it was could wait at least wait until he dried off and got on some dry clothes.

Now dry and warmly dressed, with a beer in his hand, Edward glanced out the window. It was black as pitch. It seemed much later than just 7pm as he picked up his phone to place a return call to Chief Haney. But before he did, he called The Old Country Kitchen hoping to talk to Katie. He had promised the girl he would check with Chief Haney about Capt'n Petey and wanted to assure her that he tried. He also wanted to know if there was anything more she might have heard before calling the police chief back.

On the first ring, Edward heard, “Old Country Kitchen, Hunter speaking, how may I help you?”

“Oh, hey Hunter. Edward Thatcher again. I was hoping to catch Katie. Is she there tonight?”

“In fact she is sir. Let me get her for you.”

Edward heard Hunter clumsily drop the phone receiver down onto the counter. There was background chatter that Edward couldn’t make out, but after waiting about 2 minutes, Hunter picked the phone back up.

“Um, Edward. This is Hunter again. I went back to the kitchen to get Katie, but our cook said she went out the back door with some food and got into Officer Meekins squad car. He wasn't sure where they were headed.”

“Would you have any idea why she would have left with Officer Meekins?” Edward asked.

“Well, no sir. Not for sure. I mean, sometimes if the Chief has a prisoner, we’ll provide meals for them. But Katie wouldn’t deliver it herself. Officer Meekins would just come in and pick it up as a to go order.”

“Hunter, any way of knowing if Officer Meekins or Chief Haney would have called a to go order in?”

“Yes sir, we keep track of those in a notebook so we can bill those meals to the city. If you don’t mind holding another second I can run back to the office and check the book.”

“I don’t mind holding at all. Thank you Hunter,” Edward replied.

After another couple of minutes on hold, Hunter returned to the phone. “Well this sure is strange Edward.”

“What is Hunter?” Edward asked.

“Well, Katie did make a food entry here for the prison cell.”

“Why is that strange then?”

“It’s not so much that we provided a meal that is strange. It’s what we provided.”

“How’s that Hunter?”

“Well sir, when we supply a meal it's usually a cheeseburger and fries, or a salad. That kind of thing.”

“This order wasn't that?”

“No. This was an order for a T-bone steak, fries, grilled asparagus, a side salad and a piece of apple pie.”

After a second or two spent contemplating what Hunter just said, Edward said, “Well, Hunter, maybe that was just the Chief’s dinner. I know he’s working late tonight. In fact, he just left me a message a few minutes ago. Perhaps he figured it would be a late night and he wanted some dinner.”

“I don’t think that’s it sir.” Hunter responded.

“Why do you say that?”

“I thought maybe that might be what it was too, but we have a separate book for Chief Haney. Sometimes he does order to go food too. But we bill him separately from the city. He pays for his own meals and then expenses them back on his own. I checked his book. There is nothing in there for tonight.”

Another few seconds of dead air went by before Edward picked the conversation back up again.

“Maybe Katie just wrote it in the wrong book.” Edward offered as an explanation.

“Nah, Edward. Katie, she doesn't make mistakes like that. Besides, even if she did, why would she be delivering it instead of Officer Meekins taking it back?”

“You got me there son.” Edward answered. “Like I mentioned, Chief Haney left me a voice mail a little bit ago. Let me try calling him. Perhaps then we can get to the bottom of this.”

“Ok sir. And if anything comes up, I have your number. Either I or Katie will give you a call back.”

“Thanks Hunter. I appreciate that.”

With that both parties hung up.

Chapter 16

Edward didn't like the feeling he was getting deep into the pit of his stomach. First, all this Teach's Light phoney baloney, then Capt'n Petey disappears without a trace. And while researching the family, Edward finds out his father had a brother, two years older, that he may or may not have known about, and who was given up at birth. Now Katie goes off on her own without a word to anyone with a fancy meal all packed up. Then there's the 6 missed calls from Chief Haney with one cryptic voice mail. Oh, and let's not forget about the sand cave that seems to run under his house!

Edward picked his phone back up, dialing the non-emergency number for the Bath Police Department.

"Bath PO-Lease. Officer Meekins."

"Hi Officer Meekins, Edward Thatcher here."

"Oh hey Mr Thatcher. I told the chief you'd called earlier. Not sure if he called you back. Said he would."

"Yes, Officer." Edward replied. "He called me back. Thank you."

"Yes sir. What more kin I do fer ya?"

"Is the chief there? He left me a message."

"Yes sir. He's here. He be in the back with the girl from the diner. They feedin' the prisoner I expect."

"Who's the prisoner Officer Meekins" Edward wanted to know.

"I reckon I can't tell ya that, Mr Thatcher. Privacy stuff and all that."

"No worries. Just being nosy. Anyway, the chief wanted me to call him back. Can he be interrupted?"

"I expect he can. Let me find out fer ya."

No doubt without holding his hand over the speaking part of the phone receiver, Edward heard the officer yell out: "Hey Chief. It's that Thatcher feller on da phone. Said you wanted to jaw at 'im."

Edward didn't hear the chief's reply, but a few seconds later someone picked up the phone…

.

"Mr Thatcher. This here's Chief Haney."

"Hi Chief. Looks like you really been trying hard to get a hold of me tonight."

"Yes sir. I expect I have. We have a, uh, what I guess you, um, could call a little situation here in town. I hate to ask you this, but I need you to come back here for some pressing business."

"Well chief, my magazine deadline is in a few days. I'm not sure I can shake away any time this week. Can you tell me what it's about?"

"Well sir," The chief began. "I don't mean to put any undue hardship on you, especially now, having just recently burying your paw and all. But I'm afraid, this can't really wait a week. And its not something I can talk to you about over the phone."

The chief heard Edward sigh loudly into the phone before continuing. "There's been a break-in of your family home and I need you to come down and sign out a complaint or at least take your statement. Plus, you'll likely be wanting to fix the basement window before animals start making their way in and calling your house their home."

"Ok chief. I don't like it, but I'll figure something out in my schedule. Would tomorrow late afternoon work?"

“Yes sir. We’ll make that work Mr Thatcher. Again, I don’t mean to make any undue hardship on you. But I suspect you’ll be glad you made the trip.”

“If you say so chief” Edward said, not very convincingly. “Oh, say chief?”

“Yes sir?”

“Officer Meekins. He said Katie from the diner was at the jail. She ok?’

“Yes sir. She’s fine. And Mr Thatcher? No sense asking her nuthin’ about this. She can’t tell you either. Not until you come down here and settle a couple of issues.

“Yes chief. Thank you. I’ll see you tomorrow afternoon.”

“Thank you Mr Thatcher. And be careful driving. The roads are wet and still have standing water on them.”

“Thanks chief. I’ll be careful.”

Edward set down his phone. It was now going on 8pm. He knew that in order to get the magazine out on time and to make a return trip to Bath to attend to whatever the problem there was there, he was going to have to get an early start to the day tomorrow.

Edward grabbed another beer from the refrigerator and drank that while absentmindedly looking through the Ancestry.com email again. After a few minutes, getting frustrated for having more questions than answers, Edward slammed the lid shut on his laptop, he drained the beer and went off for what he knew would be a fitful night of sleep.

Chapter 17

After looking at the time on the clock every hour throughout the night, Edward finally decided to get up for the day at 4:30 am. As he lay in bed for just a few moments, he could still hear the wind and the rain, though it didn't sound as loud and ferocious as it had over the last several days.

Edward finally got up, turned the Keurig on to warm and then went into the bathroom, turned on the shower and waited there too for the hot water. Fifteen minutes later he was washed, dried and dressed in khaki shorts and a green "Seascape" golf shirt. Seascape being a golf course in neighboring Kitty Hawk that Edward would occasionally spend 5 hours being frustrated at about twice a month. He then packed a bag in case he was stuck for the night in Bath before coming out into the kitchen to make what was sure to be the first of many cups of coffee on this day.

Still using the door on the south side of the house, Edward, with thermos cup of coffee and overnight bag in hand, ran through the rain and the wind to the Jeep, parked in the drive. He made the short drive to the office and immediately went right to work in the upstairs prep room.

It was times like this Edward wished he could afford a graphic designer to put together the magazine. It was not Edward's forte, but he still was able to put out an esthetically pleasing magazine each month. It just took him way longer than it should.

Piece by piece, Edward grabbed the story files in the computer and formatted them to fit the magazine while placing the pictures throughout each article to accentuate the story being told. He captioned the pictures, wrote the intro's to each story and checked each advertisement against its contract to make sure their size and content was correct. He then placed the ads in their proper place in the magazine, making sure that competing businesses didn't end up on the same page. He even proof read each to ensure there were no errors. Edward didn't want any mistakes.

About 4 hours into the set up of the publication, Edward heard noises coming from the downstairs office. Noticing that it was almost 9, Edward knew it would be Char and Billy coming in for the day.

Even though she had seen the Jeep in the parking lot, and figuring Edward to be in working on the set up prior to the deadline, Char was startled when Edward came down the stairs.

"A little jumpy this morning?" Edward asked of Char.

"It's just all this rain and gloom. It has made everything depressing and hard to focus. I can't wait for the sun to make a return to the Outer Banks."

Grabbing a cup of coffee from the Keurig, Edward replied with "me too Char. Me too."

Grabbing some hot water for a tea, Char asked Edward "What brings you in so early? Judging by the looks of you, you've been here for a while."

Edward recounted his phone call from Chief Haney from the previous day. Knowing that he'd lose a lot of time, he decided to come in to get a jump on the magazine layout.

"When you leaving boss?" Billy chirped in as he came from his office.

"Well, I'm guessing with the weather being what it is, I better get a start soon. I really don't want to be stuck in Bath again tonight. I want to do what I have to do and be home in my own bed tonight. Then back in here tomorrow morning to finish getting the magazine ready."

"Anything you need us to do while gone?" Char asked.

"Just keep the lights burning by re-upping some ads for next month if you would. Maybe hit Ocean 105 to see if they'd be interested in bartering out some advertising. We'll give them an ad for some radio time."

"Will do Edward." Char replied.

"Anything for me chief?" Asked Billy.

"Actually, yes. I'd really like to do a feature story next month on the Beach Food Pantry. Can you give them a call and talk to them. Everyone talks to them just before the holidays, I want a slant on the story that says, you don't have to wait for the holidays to help those in need."

"Got it," Billy replied.

With that, Edward drained the rest of his coffee from his cup and poured more into his thermos cup and ran back out in the elements and to his Jeep.

The roads off the beach and onto the mainland weren't as bad as Edward figured them to be. Even with rain and wind that has blown virtually non-stop for over a week, the roads were relatively clear. Not much traffic either. Weather like this tends to keep people from traveling unless there's an absolute need. Edward decided to take the southerly route back to Bath, not wanting to chance on there being a problem with the Alligator Bridge, as there often times is.

It only took about 2 1/2 hours for Edward to make it to town, and he went straight to the police department to see Chief Haney. He jumped out of the Jeep and ran up the 6 steps to the front of the police station, taking them two at a time. Edward pulled open the large glass plate door with the brass handle and shook the rain off himself as he went inside. Off to his left, Edward noticed a tall, almost painfully thin police officer with a large Adam's apple and very weak chin sitting behind a large oak desk.

Noticing the name tag on the officer's uniform, Edward said, “Hello Officer Meekins. I'm here to see Chief Haney.”

Officer Meekins, seemingly bored with life at that moment replied, “Well sir, its lunchtime. Chief's grabbin' some grub 'bout now. He expectin' ya?”

“He is officer. But likely not till later this afternoon. I got on the road a bit earlier than I thought I would.”

“Oh, you must be that Thatcher feller. Yeah. He be expectin' you later.”

“Well, would you know where I might reach him? I'd like to get things wrapped up. I need to get taken care of, whatever needs taken care of and get back to the Outer Banks today. I'd like to do that before dark if I can.”

“Well sir. Sometimes the chief, he goes home fer lunch. Other days, he goes over to the Country Kitchen. Sometimes his missus, she packs him a lunch that he eats at his desk. But she didn't do 'dat today. He left outta here.”

Getting a bit impatient now, Edward asked as nicely as he could, “Well Officer Meekins, can we call him to find out where he is? That way I can meet him there?”

Rubbing his chin with his right hand, as though he was thinking what he should do, Officer Meekins finally said, “Sir, the chief, he don’t like being disturbed while he got his feed bag on. He gets more ornery than a grizzle bear when he is, but I reckon he be waitin’ on you to git here, so maybe he’d be ok fer me to call.”

“Thank you officer. I truly appreciate that.”

Officer Meekins picked up the phone sitting on his right and dialed a number. And waited. After several seconds he said to Edward “Well sir, I don’t reckon he gonna answer me.”

Before Edward could answer back, Officer Meekins said into the phone, “Hey chief, this be Drew. I knowed you don’t want to be bothered while ya be eatin’, but this Thatcher feller be here and wanted me to call ya.”

With that, the officer set the phone back into its cradle.

“What did he say officer?” Edward asked.

“Nothin’.”

“What do you mean nothing? He must have said something!”

“No sir. I’d left a message fer him. The chief, he didn’t answer.”

Feeling frustrated, and a bit hungry since he left the beach without having eaten anything yet that day, Edward told Officer Meekins that he was going to head over to the Country Kitchen to grab a sandwich and would be right back. And as he was opening the plate glass door to go back outside, Edward looked back over his shoulder and said to the police officer, “Please Officer Meekins, if the chief gets back before I do, don’t let him leave. I’m just going to grab my lunch to go.”

“Yes sir....”

Not feeling particularly confident that Officer Meekins quite understood his directions, or even cared that he was on a tight schedule, Edward spun the Jeep's tires in the gravel parking lot as he threw it into gear and turned right out onto the street in the direction of the Country Kitchen.

Edward's family home was between the police station and the Country Kitchen. As he drove past, he noticed some police crime scene tape covering the southwest corner of the house. He stopped, got out of the Jeep, and tried to inspect the area for what had happened. All he could ascertain was that someone had busted out a basement window. At least the police, or someone, jammed a piece of wood board into the opening in the house to keep out both the weather and any animals. Thinking it was probably just neighborhood kids knowing the house was empty, and looking for a place to drink beer, Edward got back into his Jeep.

A few seconds later, Edward was standing at the hostess stand at the Country Kitchen. They were in the middle of their lunch rush and it was close to five minutes before a restaurant worker even noticed he was standing there. During the wait, Edward looked around the room for the police chief. He wasn't there. Must of gone home for lunch Edward thought. Edward saw neither Katie or Hunter either. The employee that finally greeted him was one he hadn't noticed before. The name tag indicated her name was Kourtney.

"Just one for lunch?" Kourtney asked.

"Uh. Yes. I mean no." Edward replied. "I was looking for either Katie or Hunter. Either one here today?"

"I wish!. This place is bananas. Fine time for them to take a day off. But you know, when your parents own the place you kinda call the shots. I'm just the cousin. I don't get no special treatment."

"Ah, I see," Edward said. Figuring that ordering something pre-made might be quicker, plus it would also help ease cousin Kourtney's stress, Edward continued, "Can I just grab a to go bowl of chili and a coffee please?"

"That's it?"

"Yep Kourtney. That will do it."

"Ok. Coming right up."

Kourtney took a couple of steps to the kitchen and yelled out "One gas maker and a hot joe on the fly please!"

Kourtney rang up the order totaling $8.72 and gave Edward his change back from a $20. She ran back to the kitchen, bagged up the order and Edward was on his way back to the police station a mere 10 minutes after leaving.

As he got out of his Jeep and made his way inside the station, he noticed Officer Meekins picking up the phone. He also noticed him hanging it back up again, before dialing a number. It was the police officer who spoke first…

"Mr Thatcher, the chief, he got my message. Weren't too happy about it neither, with him bein' at lunch and all. I was just 'bout to call ya."

"I'm sorry he was upset with you officer, but what did the chief have to say?"

"Well sir. Said he was sorry he missed ya. Weren't expectin' ya till later. But he said he'd be back by quarter to 2 and to tell you to wait fer 'im."

Looking at the clock on the far wall, Edward noticed that it was just after 1. Only have less than an hour wait.

"Ok officer," Edward said. "Don't suppose you can tell me what this is all about, can you?"

“I don’t rightly know myself. I knowed we got a prisoner in da back and he did somethin’ to yer house. But don’t know what.”

“Do you know who this prisoner is officer?”

“Nah, sir. The chief, he told me not to go back there.”

“Aren’t you just a little curious who it is officer?”

“Nah, Mr. Thatcher. See? I did somethin’ once the chief told me not to do. Well, I almost got fired fer it. And I got a wife at home and 3 younguns too. Not to mention my wife’s 5 dang cats. This here da best job a feller can git and I’m not gonna lose it ‘cause you want to know who the prisoner be.”

“I get that officer. I don’t want you to get into any trouble with your chief. I’ll just sit over here and eat my chili and wait for the chief if that’s ok with you.”

“Yes sir. That chili smells awful powerful good. That from the Country Kitchen?

“It is. Would you like some?”

“Nah, but I thank ya. Next payday, I’m gonna bring some of that chili home to the wife and younguns. Surprise them, ya know?”

“Sounds like a mighty fine surprise to me officer.”

Chapter 18

It was 1:52 when Chief Haney finally got back to the police station from lunch. By this time Edward was quite a bit antsy, wanting to know what was going on and when he might be able to get back on the road home for the beach. Having not seen each other face-to-face since Edward was a young kid heading off to college up in Chapel Hill, and not recognizing him sitting in the lobby, the chief blew right past Edward and went into his office, slamming the door behind him.

Edward stood and approached Officer Meekins. “Was that the Chief?” He asked.

“Yes sir.” The officer replied.

“He not see me?”

“Don’t rightly know.”

“Can you *please* let the chief know I’m here?” Edward asked, emphasizing the word please.

Officer Meekins picked up the phone, hit an extension and into the phone said, “Chief, that Thatcher feller is here and he’d be in a hurry to see you.”

After a few seconds the officer hung up the phone and said to Edward, “The chief, he said he’d be right out. He wanted to check in on the prisoner ‘afore seein’ ya. He told me to see if you wanted some coffee while you be waitin’ here.”

“No thanks officer, I just want to see the chief.”

“Yes sir. He’d be here in a second.”

Edward paced the lobby in the police station, while waiting on the chief. He wasn’t one for sitting anyway. He’s always been a pacer. Char always jokingly said it was ADHD, Edward often wondered if she was right.

It was 5 minutes later, when the chief's office door opened. Chief Haney, stood nearly 6 foot 3 with a slight paunch around his middle. His hair was shaved close to the head. The once jet black hair, being over taken by the gray that had been creeping in.

"Mr Thatcher, so sorry to have kept you waiting," the chief said with his hand outstretched.

"That's ok chief. As you can imagine I'm a little bit confused as to why I'm here."

"Yes. I'm sure you are, and for that I apologize. It's kind of a delicate situation that really needed your presence. Before we sit down, let me once again express my condolences to you on your maw and paw. Really nice people. So sad that they're both gone."

"Thank you chief. Sometimes its hard to comprehend that they're both gone," Edward responded.

"Please, Mr Thatcher, let's go into my office where you'll be more comfortable. Can Officer Meekins get you anything? Water? Coffee?"

"No thank you chief. I just want to get to the bottom of what is going on. I'm hoping to get back to the beach tonight. I still have a magazine to put out."

"Yes of course. Hopefully this will only take a short time."

Chief Haney led Edward into his office. The chief sat behind his rather large mahogany desk and motioned to Edward to sit in one of the two leather chairs positioned in front of the desk. Edward noticed immediately that the chief had the levels of the chairs set so the chief sat nearly a foot higher than anyone sitting in front of him. All of a sudden he became a much more imposing figure than he already was at 6 foot 3.

It was the chief who spoke first. “Well, Mr Thatcher, again, sorry for all the cloak and dagger stuff, but we do have a situation here that normally wouldn’t require your physical presence. We would just book the subject and let the courts take it from there. But because this is a little different a situation, I needed you here to help me untangle it.”

“Well chief, of course I’m happy to help if I can, but I’m not sure what I can do.”

“Mr Thatcher, let’s start at the beginning and we’ll see exactly how you can help.”

“Sure chief.”

“As you might expect, we are a fairly small police department here in Bath. Really, a lot of the policing is done by Beaufort County Sheriff’s Department, but we do what we can right here in town. One of the things that Officer Meekins and I do is to patrol the town to ensure everyone is safe. Keep an eye on the properties, especially the vacant ones.” With that, the chief reached over to his right and grabbed the coffee cup that was already sitting there. He took a long, careful sip before continuing.

“Well, Mr Thatcher, it was in the process of checking on properties that we noticed the broken basement window at your folks home. At first, we didn’t know if maybe, a garbage can or some other object was blown into the glass during the wind storm causing it to break, or if there was a trespasser.”

“I’m guessing since I’m sitting here talking to you that it wasn’t a flying garbage can.”

“No sir, Mr Thatcher. It wasn’t.”

“I’m also guessing that whomever is the prisoner you have in back, is the person you caught trespassing on my family’s property.”

"Yes sir," the chief replied. "And again, normally we would just prosecute, but this trespasser had a very unusual tale to tell. Said he had a right to be there."

Edward didn't say anything for a few seconds. He then said, "Had a right? Chief, with my parents gone and now in the church cemetery, only I have a right to be there. No one else."

"Yeah. That's what I kinda figured too. Maybe you should hear this feller's story and we can go from there."

"Yes chief. That sounds like a mighty fine idea. Let's get this settled so I can get back on the road for home."

Chapter 19

Edward got up from his chair as Chief Haney led him out the back door of the office into a hallway. From there they turned right into the area that housed two cells. The first occupied by someone Edward didn't recognize. But judging by the prisoner's appearance, he was there sleeping off an early morning drunk. The second cell also contained a prisoner. This one was laying on his cot, facing the far wall. At first Edward didn't recognize him, but something about him was familiar. As the chief, reached for the key and opened the cell door, the prisoner was startled awake, rolled over and looked into Edward's eyes.

"Me boy. It is a might good to see you again." The prisoner said.

Also startled, Edward replied, "Capt'n Petey. What in the world is going on? I am so glad you're ok. Me and Katie over at the diner, we've been worried about you during the storm."

"Aw boy, no need to worry 'bout this ol' capt'n. I can always take care of m'self."

Edward, now directing his attention to Chief Haney, "Chief, is this who you arrested for breaking into my house?"

Capt'n Petey, looking a bit embarrassed by the whole situation spoke before the chief had a chance. "Yeah boy. He got me red-handed. It were me that broke yer window to go inside to get m'self warm and dry. But I figured your paw, he wouldn't have minded, if he were still around. Bless his soul."

Chief Haney jumped into the conversation, "Mr Thatcher, when we looked around the house, we found Mr Dussault here up in your folks old bedroom sleeping. We don't doubt that he only gained entry to escape the storm. It was a bad one, but still, he broke and entered a vacant building."

“'Tis true me boy. The chief, he caught me and I’m awfully sorry about that broke window. I’ll pay for it......somehow.”

“Capt’n Petey, chief, I don’t care about a broken window. I’m just glad the captain is safe. If you needed a place to stay, of course I would have let you stay in the house. But why didn’t you just call me and ask?”

Sheepishly the captain replied, “Son, I don’t want to be no burden to you. Your maw and your paw, they’d be nice to the ol’ capt’n, but you don’t knowed me from Adam. I didn’t want to be no charity case, neither. Plus, I didn’t think no one would even knowed I was there.”

Interrupting the conversation Chief Haney interjected “Mr Dussault, why don’t you tell Mr Thatcher here what you told me. You know, about having a right to be there and all.”

“Now chief, I don’t know I can tell the boy that. Not yet anyway. Might not be the time.”

“Tell me what Capt’n?” Edward wanted to know.

“Chief, mind if I have a cup of that hot coffee ‘afore I tell the boy what you're askin’ me to say?” Captain Petey asked.

Chief Haney excused himself for a brief moment to grab three cups of coffee. One for each man. The prisoner in cell one, woken up from his drunken sleep from the conversation in the neighboring cell complaining that he didn’t get one.

“Ok Mr Dussault,” Chief Haney said. “Why don’t you tell Mr Thatcher here what you told me?”

“Ok chief, I reckon I better,” Capt’n Petey began. “My boy, ‘member I told you that your paw and me, we kindly took care of each other.”

“Yes I remember that conversation at breakfast that one morning,” Edward replied.

"Well we did. But it turns out that it were more than just two old codgers finding friendship outta loneliness. Just 'afore your maw died, your paw found out somethin' that he and me didn't know."

"What's that Capt'n Petey?" Edward asked.

"Turns out your maw, she'd be pushing your paw into talking to you about the family, even more than usual. Just 'afore she passed, she find out that your paw and me, we'd be brothers."

"Yes, Mr Thatcher. That's why Mr Dussault said he had a right to being in the house when we found him there," Chief Haney interjected.

"Wait, what?" Edward replied.

"Your paw and me. We be brothers. Neither of us knowed that until just before Pam, I mean, your maw died."

Instantly Edward's mind flashed back to the Ancestry.com email. Edward Thatcher Senior had a brother, given up for adoption two years before Edward senior was born. Sure, P.E. Thatcher. Pete E. Thatcher!

"Capt'n Petey," Edward blurted out. "Your middle initial, it wouldn't be E, would it?"

"Yes boy, it be E for Edward. How you'd know?"

"Capt'n Petey, my mother wasn't the only one doing research, I too have been doing some research on the family from home on the beach. I found out my dad had a brother that was adopted and the only thing listed was P.E. Thatcher. I'm guessing you're P.E Thatcher."

"Sorta my boy. I really be P.E Dussault. The Dussualt's were the people that raised the ol' capt'n. Raised me to be a fisherman. But, you'd be right. I reckon I was born Thatcher. Yer maw and yer paw and me, we don't rightly know why I was done given up. Likely 'cause the Thatchers didn't have no money for no youngun, or maybe my maw and paw weren't married yet. Different times, you know."

Turning his attention back to the police chief, Edward said, "Chief, if you asked me here to see if I was going to press charges, well I'm not."

"I kinda figured that Mr Thatcher. Again, I'm sorry to have inconvenienced you by asking you to come back to town, but I'm sure now you understand why."

"I do indeed chief. Thank you," Edward responded. "Is it ok for me to take Capt'n Petey out of here now?"

"Yes sir. I will release him into your custody and we'll mark the case closed saying you didn't want to press breaking and entering charges."

"Thank you chief." Edward replied.

As Capt'n Petey, Chief Haney and Edward walked back to the front of the police station to leave, the prisoner in cell 1, still apparently feeling the effects of his stupor yelled out, "Hey boy. Your pappy and me, we be brothers too! Take me home too!"

"Pipe down Otis, just pipe down!" Chief Haney said as Edward left the police station with Captain Petey in tow.

Chapter 20

"Capt'n Petey," Edward started the conversation as the two walked out of the building and onto the street, "do you not have a place to stay?"

"Well my boy, not exactly at the moment. See, I was livin' on the boat I was captainin', but the owner, he retired me and he didn't know I be livin' there. It not be as bad as you might think. I don't mind campin' out in the woods. Gettin' back to nature, you know? It be good fer the body and good fer the soul too. But, this blow, it be mean and nasty. I was soaked to the bone and uh, well, the ol' capt'n, he just wanted to get warm and dry fer a bit."

"Capt'n Petey, I want you to stay at the house. Especially now that I know we're family. No more camping out in the woods! Besides….." and before Edward could continue Captain Petey interrupted him.

"No, sir!" Captain Petey said loudly. "No sir! I ain't no charity case! This ol' captain, he can take care of 'hiself!"

"Cap'n Petey," Edward replied. "Let me finish before you go getting all proud and full of yourself."

"Sorry boy, but Ol' Capt'n Petey, he ain't no charity case."
"I know you're not and I'm not suggesting that you are, but what I was going to say was, I want you staying at the house, not for charity reasons but because I need a caretaker."

"How do you mean, my boy?" Captain Petey asked.

"Well, as I told you earlier, I don't know what I'm going to do with the house. I mean, I've thought about selling it, but that just doesn't seem right. My parents worked hard maintaining this home for themselves and me. But being up in Nags Head, I didn't know how I was going to maintain it. If I did that, I was going to have to find someone who I could trust that would make sure the grass was always cut, that there wasn't any water leaks that would go undetected until it was too late. Someone that could bring in any mail that might still arrive. Bills for utilities. Things like that. The problem is, I didn't know who I could trust to do all that for me."

"Whatcha gettin' at boy?"

"Seems obvious to me Capt'n Petey. I'd have someone here who I could trust to take care of all those things. And you would have a warm, dry place to lay your head every night."

"No charity then boy?"

"No charity Capt'n. In fact I would have to pay you some sort of small salary for doing those things for me."

"A salary too?"

"Yes Capt'n," Edward replied. "A salary too. No matter who I would have gotten to watch the place, I was going to have to pay them anyway. Why not pay you? You are kin after all."

"Boy, you don't know the ol' capt'n from no one. Why you gonna trust me? We'd just meet a little bit ago."

"Captain, I know all about you that I need to know," Edward responded. "Firstly, you're family. Now I don't know what that means to the Dussault family, but it means something to the Thatchers. Secondly, you took care of my dad when I wasn't around. Thirdly, my ma knew you too. And if she liked you, well, then you're alright as far as I'm concerned."

“I don’t know what to say my boy. This ol’ capt’n, he ain’t never at a loss for no words, but he surely is now.”

“Just say you’ll be the family home caretaker.”

“I’ll do it my boy. I’ll do it fer you. I do it fer yer maw and yer paw. I’ll look after their graves fer you too.”

“Captain, there is one other thing before this thing is a done deal.”

“What that my boy?”

“Capt’n Petey, I have this nagging feeling that you haven’t told me everything about this family. I suspect you know some things that maybe my dad and you have talked about. Things that you said I can’t know right now.”

“I might boy. I just might….”

“Alright, here’s the deal. I don’t want you to betray anything you told my mom or my dad, but when you determine when the time is right, I want to sit down with you and learn all you know.”

“Aye, my boy. I reckon the ol’ captain, can do that fer you. No charge on that one.”

Both men laughed hard at that as they got in the Jeep and headed for the family home on King Street.

Chapter 21

After a trip to the grocery store for much needed food for the house Edward asked, "Captain Petey, you all settled in enough?"

"Aye boy. Reckon I am at that."

Fishing through his wallet, Edward pulled out all that he had, 5 twenty dollar bills and 3 singles. "Here you go Capt'n," Edward said as he put the cash into Captain Petey's hand. "Here's $128 to tide you over till I get back to the beach and send you some more."

"Boy, you just bought me groceries, you don't need to give me no cash now."

"I want you to have this on hand Captain Petey. If you don't need it, don't use it. But I want you to have it just in case. Now, I can't come out here very week to give you cash, and I can't send cash in the mail, and I know you don't have a bank account...."

Looking at the ground embarrassed, Captain Petey replied, "No boy. Never trusted a bank. Plus, I ain't never had enough cash at one time to put in a bank."

"No worries," Edward continued. "I'll send you a check every Friday so you'll have it every Monday. I already called Katie down at the Old Country Kitchen. You sign the back of the check and take it to her. She will cash it for you at the restaurant."

"Boy, I don't need no money EVERY week," the captain protested. "I've done alright not knowin' when I would get money again."

"Yes, captain, I realize that. But now you don't have to not know when you'll get money again. If you don't need the money, then you don't need to take the check down to Katie. I'll let you decide that."

"Sounds fair to me boy."

Glancing at his watch and noticing it was now close to 5pm, Edward was antsy to get back on the road to get the magazine finished up and off to the printers. "Here's my phone number Capt'n Petey. You need anything you just call me."

"I will boy. You just know that ol' Capt'n Petey here, he'll be takin' real good care of yer house. I'll plant flowers on your folks grave too. Make it all nice and pretty for when you come fer a visit."

"Thanks Captain. I sure would appreciate that. My folks deserve that."

Edward put out his hand to shake Captain Petey's. "Ok capt'n Petey, or should I call you Uncle Petey?"

"I done been capt'n fer more years than I remember. Let us just leave it at capt'n."

"Yes sir Capt'n Petey, "Edward replied.

The two men hugged good-bye. Edward started for the front door to begin his trip back to the Outer Banks and as he was about to close the door, Edward looked back into the house just in time to see Captain P. E. Dussault wipe a tear from his eye. As he closed the door, Edward did the same.

Chapter 22

The sun had set about an hour and a half before Edward got back home to his little beach box on Virginia Dare Trail in Nags Head across from the Lucky 12 Tavern. The wind still buffeting him most of the way. Still blowing from the Northeast in double digits, just as it has for nearly two weeks now. Thankfully, the weather forecast was calling for the end of the blow in the next day or so. This had been one of the longest Nor'easter that anyone could remember. The last time one blew this hard and this long, was well before anyone currently living on the Outer Banks was alive. In fact that blow came just days following the Civil War Battle of Hatteras Inlet in late August of 1861. At least, that's what the news guy said on the radio.

Before pulling into his driveway, Edward stopped at the Kentucky Fried Chicken at Whalebone Junction to grab some dinner. He only had that to go chili and was a bit hungry. Well aware that he ate nothing but garbage today, he vowed to work off the food with a long, hard swim at the YMCA the next day, should time allow for it.

Turning on the television, it was still on the Weather Channel. Edward watched for a bit while eating his three-piece chicken dinner with mashed potatoes and cole slaw, washing it down with a Lost Colony Blonde Ale.

Not really paying attention until the Weather Channel news anchor threw it out to a reporter in Nags Head. The reporter, whose name Edward didn't catch, was reporting from the Nags Head Pier. What he heard was….

"The Sheriff's Department continues to warn people to stay away from the sand escarpment that has formed near milepost 11 here in Nags Head. The size of which as grown a great deal in the last 24 hours. The danger lies, not in the rain and the surf, but in the direction of the wind. The escarpment will completely disappear in the next 24 -36 hours when the winds shift from the northeast to the southwest. It will smooth the sand out and will likely bury anything in its way. Reporting from Nags Head...."

Edward flipped off the television. Too late and too dark now to go back out to investigate. Maybe at first light, Edward thought.

It had been a long day. Edward thought that a good night sleep would be just what the doctor ordered. He's likely going to have another long day tomorrow, getting the rest of the magazine together, having lost a day on it because of his trip to Bath.

Edward, still in the clothes he wore that day, fell into his bed and was asleep within minutes.

Chapter 23

It came at about 2:30 in the morning. Outside of his bedroom window Edward saw the bright light out over the Atlantic Ocean. The same light that he saw in Bath several days ago. It just hovered, not fluctuating from the stiff northeast wind. It startled Edward awake, just as it had before.

Edward jumped up from his bed and ran outside and climbed up the sand dune behind the house owned by the Florida couple. Just as he got to the crest of the dune, the light disappeared. Just like that......gone!

Edward walked slowly back to his house, looking back over his shoulder several times for any clue as to what the light might have been. But he knew. Edward knew it was Captain Teach. But why he appeared here, at this time, Edward wasn't sure.

Getting back to sleep that night proved much harder than it had been the first time. Edward not being able to turn off his brain. Questions. Almost always questions. Never any answers. Well, one answer anyway. The mystery of P. E. Thatcher has at least been solved. But not much else.

It was about 5:30 in the morning when Edward decided to get up with the sun. He looked back in the direction of the ocean to see if there was anything more he could figure out from last night's appearance of Blackbeard's ghost. Nothing. Edward went back outside. The sun, making more of an appearance than it had over the course of the last couple of weeks. The wind from the northeast slacking much more than it had the night before. It might just be the first nice day on the Outer Banks since leaving for his father's funeral.

Edward went back outside to the sand dune. The escarpment much more severe than it had been two days ago when he last inspected it. Carefully Edward made his way down to the beach, the same way he had before. Walking down the wooden walkway to the gazebo at the vacant vacation house south of his. He climbed over the railing walked to the gazebo and made his way down the stairs to where he jumped back down to the beach.

Making his way back north, with the sand escarpment on his left and the angry waters of the gray Atlantic Ocean on his right, Edward walked until he found the opening to the sand cave that he had seen a couple of days prior. The entrance now much larger and much wider than it was before. With the words of the Weather Channel reporter, echoing through his head...."the wind will smooth out the sand and bury anything in its path...." Edward carefully peered into the opening of the cave. As you might expect, the further in, the darker it was. Edward took a half step into the entrance of the cave. Then he took a full step. Then a second step. Before he knew it Edward found himself about 10 yards into the cave.

Off to his right Edward saw a corridor in the cave. In the back of the corridor was a flickering light. Why would there be a light in a cave formed by Mother Nature, Edward wondered. Forgetting now about the danger as curiosity got the best of him. Edward walked softly and slowly to the right. About 20 more yards in, the corridor turned sharply to the left. Edward followed the turn and with each step taken, he felt like he was walking back in the direction of his home on the Beach Road.

Wishing he had a flashlight, Edward used the next best thing. He reached for his cell phone in his back left pocket. He pressed the flashlight app on the phone and pointed it forward as he continued to walk slowly toward the back of the sand cave.

The corridor started slanting down as Edward walked further, deeper into the cave. The hill getting steeper and steeper the further he went. Edward estimated that he walked about the length of a football field into the cave. The distance and the angle downward made it feel as though he was right about underneath his house.

One more bend in the corridor, where the light that he had seen from the entrance to the cave was emitting a very bright light. Just a few minutes ago Edward wished he had his flashlight, now he could have used his sunglasses, it was that bright.

Again, at the moment, curiosity outweighed safety as Edward moved s-l-o-wl-y toward the light. He rounded the corner and found himself in a large room of the sand cave. The light so bright it took him several seconds to focus. When he did, he stood there paralyzed with fear. The light that he saw from the entrance of the sand cave was burning as bright as anything he had ever seen. It didn't come from a lamp or a torch, but rather it was the light he had seen the night before.......and several days before that in Bath.

Edward saw nothing but the light for a long while. It just hovered. It didn't move. It didn't flicker. It just hovered in place, remaining the same white, bright image. Slowly, Edward took his eyes off it and looked around the room. Off to his right, he couldn't believe what he saw. Surely his eyes were playing a trick on him! It couldn't be real.......could it?

As a child he had seen pictures of it. Everyone had. And a lot of people went in search of it. They searched in Bath. They searched on Ocracoke Island. They searched points along the Spanish Main. But there it was. Right there in front of Edward, seemingly right below his house! It was Blackbeard's Treasure!

It was just like you've seen in all the movies. A wooden chest, top opened with jewels and gold crowns and coins spilling out and onto the floor. But interestingly enough, that wasn't what caught Edward's attention first. No, what caught his attention was an old, dusty, musty book lying under a bed of gold Spanish Doubloons that spilled out from the treasure chest. Edward reached for it, the light shining even brighter now as he lifted it from the stack of coins. Carefully, he pulled the book out as the light grew even brighter. The light that had to be Teach's light, Edward reasoned. There guarding the treasure that he has kept buried for 300 years.

As Edward held the ancient book, the walls began to rumble. The whole cave seemed to shake. Remembering that the escarpment was all going to go away in a matter of hours, Edward thought it prudent to get out of the cave as quickly as his legs would carry him.

Taking the book with him, Edward ran from the large room contained within the sand cave. Just as he took the left out of the room and started up the incline of the corridor and back out onto the beach, the large room behind him went dark. Edward heard a strange maniacal laugh as he continued back out of the cave. With each step he took, more of the cave behind him started to shake and collapse. Finally, in less than half the time it took him to go in, Edward made it back to the beach where he noticed a strong southwest wind was now blowing, already smoothing out the sand encampment. Running down the beach to the south, Edward got back up to the Nags Head Pier and out to the Beach Road. And just as he had, a couple of days before, Edward walked back to his house from there.

Chapter 24

Edward sat the musty book down on his desk in his office. Fired up the Keurig and sat down to study it with a cup of hot, fresh coffee. The book had to be several hundred years old, judging by what he knew of Blackbeard. The pages were very brittle and Edward was careful turning each. The thing that amazed Edward the most about the book was that it appeared to be a Bible. Why in the world would a blood-thirsty pirate, known the world over for his cruelty, be in possession of a Bible stashed with his treasure?

Finishing his coffee and making another, as he studied every page of the book when he was startled back to reality by the ringing of his cell phone. It was Char calling from the office.

"Hey Char...." Edward answered.

"Oh hey boss. Just wonderin', you in today or still in Bath?"

Edward looked at his watch and noticed it to be after 10am. "Oh, sorry Char. Time has gotten away from me. No, I'm home. Got in last night."

"Everything go ok in Bath?"

"Yeah. Long story. I'll fill you in when I get there. I'll be in within the hour."

"Roger that Edward. Billy and I are proofing now the articles that you already mocked up. We'll have those finished by the time you get in."

"Thanks Char. See you in a bit."

Edward set his cell phone down and turned his attention back to the Bible. There was some writing on the back inside cover. Written in Old English from what Edward could tell. While he couldn't make it out completely, the handwriting seemed awfully familiar to him.

Edward placed the ancient book very carefully into the top drawer of his desk, wanting to make sure no damage comes to it. He went into the bathroom to take a quick shower before heading into the magazine. While in the shower, his thoughts drifted to the treasure chest laden with riches buried deep in the sand. Maybe right there under his own house. Or at least close to it. What should he do about it. If he says anything, for sure a bunch of treasure hunters will descend down on his property and he won't have a moments peace. Back in the days of the gold rush, prospectors would stake a claim. Is that what you still do in the 21st century? Edward didn't know.

Edward climbed out of the shower. He toweled off and got dressed. Before leaving for the magazine he opened the desk drawer again, just to make sure he wasn't dreaming about the book. He wasn't. It was sitting exactly where he left it, beneath a pile of paperwork.

Edward left the house for work. He noticed how nice of a day it had turned out to be. The sun was out, finally! The wind was soft and gentle out of the southwest. The sea birds were back flying overhead, as were the line of pelicans that flew along the shore, looking for their midday snack. Edward got into the Jeep and before throwing it into reverse to pull out of the driveway and onto the Beach Road, he noticed the sand dune behind the Florida couple's home had already flattened out significantly. No doubt covering back over the entrance to the cave that was just there a few hours ago.

In 5 minutes Edward found himself parking the Jeep in the lot at the magazine. A lot of the puddles and streams of water were already drying out from the sun and from the southwest wind. A completely different kind of day on the Outer Banks than it had been the last couple of weeks. Edward wasn't sure if it was the pleasant weather, or the early morning discovery, that put him in such a good mood. Likely a combination of both, he thought.

Seeing his Jeep come down the street, Char went ahead and brewed Edward a fresh cup of coffee. “Morning boss,” she said as Edward came through the door, holding out the fresh cup of coffee.

“Thanks Char,” Edward said taking a sip. “What in the world?!?!?”

Beaming from ear to ear and acting innocent, Char responded “What’s the matter Edward?”

“Cafe Bustelo? You actually broke down and got the coffee I’ve been pleading for?”

“I figure once in a while I’d throw you a bone,” Char said laughing.

“Not sure if I can get used to you actually doing what I ask!” Edward said with a smile.

Edward spent the next several minutes recanting to Char and Billy everything that transpired in Bath the previous day. Except for the part that Capt’n Petey was his uncle. Why he didn’t include that part, he wasn’t quite sure.

Once Edward’s story was finished, the three magazine employees went back up to the prep room to finish mocking up the magazine so they could get it out to the printer. Billy was placing the ads, Char proof reading everything and checking all ads against their contract, while Edward designed the articles and their pictures. Somewhere around 7 pm, having worked straight through lunch, the magazine was ready. Edward emailed the PDF’s to the printer and then treated Char and Billy to Mama Kwan’s for blackened fish tacos and a cold Lost Colony Blonde Ale for a job well done.

During dinner it was Char that had asked the question that even Edward was too scared to ask himself. “So, what will you do with the house back in Bath? You just going to hold onto it and let the old sea captain remain living there indefinitely?”

Edward waved a quick hello to a friend of his across the restaurant, thought for a second and then answered with a very confident, “I don’t know. It is just a bit more complicated than just giving an old sea captain a home.” As he said that, Edward thought to himself, much more complicated since the old sea captain was actually family.

“I would assume the mortgage is paid on it, but you still got to pay those property taxes,” Billy added.

“Not to mention utility bills” Char quickly replied.

“Yeah I know. Just seems like I can’t get rid of it right now.”

“....and the last time I knew, you weren’t exactly a rich guy,” Char threw in.

Billy threw Char one of those, “you’re going over the line again glances” that he seems to send on a daily basis to Char.

“No, I’m not exactly rich monetarily,” Edward replied. “But with friends like you Char, I’m rich in other ways.”

It was at this exact moment that the check came. Edward handed it to Char, said “you're right,” and then walked out of the restaurant to head home.

“Walked into that one,” Edward heard Char mutter as he left the table.

As he pulled open the door to leave the last thing Edward heard was Char trying to convince young Billy into at least leaving the tip.

Chapter 25

Back at home now, Edward noticed the house was a bit stuffy from being closed up the last couple of weeks. First, because he had to leave town for his father's funeral and then because of the nasty weather. Edward went around the house and opened all the windows letting in the fresh salt air breeze. He grabbed a cold Red Stripe from the refrigerator and went out and sat on the deck on the Florida couple's house.

Sultry nights like this with a cold beer in hand was one of Edward's favorite things. He sat there a while replaying everything in his mind. Teach's Light. The pirate book he had read at his parents house about Blackbeard, a wife named Mary and a forgotten son. He thought about finding P E Thatcher. And he thought about the treasure buried in the sand beneath him. How could he not think about that! But mostly he thought about that Bible he found in the cave. The Bible that the light guarding the treasure allowed him to take out of the cave. But why? He wasn't quite sure. But it felt like the light "wanted" him to take the Bible. Crazy, he thought to himself.

Knowing that Captain Petey held some answers that Edward didn't, he decided to invite the sea captain out to the beach for the weekend. Maybe they could have a discussion and Edward could figure some of those things out.

Draining the last of the Red Stripe, Edward got up from the deck. Instead of heading straight back to the house, he decided to set the empty beer bottle down on the bench of the deck and walk down to the beach. The sand escarpment was not so severe now, so he was able to get to the beach from the Florida couple's house.

Out on the beach, Edward paused a moment and looked out at the water. Not as angry as it had been the last few weeks. The moon hung over the ocean, with what seemed like a billion stars overhead. Edward turned and walked down the beach in the direction of the cave entrance. Not surprisingly, there wasn't any clue that a cave ever existed. Edward himself was not exactly sure where it once was. The dune had smoothed itself back over from the shift in winds.

Edward sat on the dune. It was quiet. More quiet than its been. No howling winds. No pelting rains. This feeling right now. This was the feeling that Edward had when he first visited the Outer Banks when he was a sophomore at UNC Chapel Hill. He, his roommate and a couple of their friends rented out a room at the Travelodge in Kill Devil Hills for a long weekend. It was then that Edward knew he would one day make the Outer Banks his home.

After a few more minutes of sitting, Edward went back to the house to call Capt'n Petey.

Chapter 26

Edward picked up his cell phone and dialed the number to his childhood home. Figuring that Capt'n Petey would be there at this time of night, Edward let it ring ten times before hanging up. Reckon I should get an answering machine for the good captain, Edward thought to himself. We'll grab one at the store when he comes into town.

Edward set down the phone and opened the desk drawer and pulled out the Blackbeard Bible. Skipping all the pages, he went straight to the back inside cover where the handwriting was that so intrigued him.

There was something about the handwriting that kept drawing him back. Edward pulled out a couple of old birthday cards that he had in his desk drawer. That's it! The handwriting was almost a perfect match to his father's! How could that even be possible, he wondered? Certainly his father hadn't seen this book before. It was buried in the sand underneath the house and Edward Senior certainly would have mentioned this, even if they were living the "Cat's in the Cradle" life. THIS WOULD HAVE COME UP IN CONVERSATION AT SOME POINT! He thought.

Edward set the book back down. He leaned back in his office chair, closed his eyes and tried putting all the pieces together in his mind. After a while Edward decided that no, this wasn't his father's handwriting. The language used was "Old English." The type used in the 1700's when America was still part of England. Edward Senior wouldn't have written anything that way.

Coincidence? Maybe. Maybe his father and the writer of the notes in the back of the Bible had similar handwriting. Not out of the realm of possibilities that two people would have similar handwriting. How many people would there have been in the world between the 1700's and now? Billions? Tens of Billions? Hundreds of Billions? Surely, out of all those people in the world, two would write similarly.

Edward's head began to hurt. He started feeling a bit sorry for himself, which was not at all his nature. If only I had taken the time to talk with my dad, before it was too late, he said to himself. I couldn't have been that busy. I could have easily found the time if I had wanted to.

Edward got up and went into the medicine cabinet in the bathroom and took two Tylenol, washing it down with another Red Stripe that he grabbed from the refrigerator.

Laying down on the bed, Edward set the beer on the nightstand, and was asleep in minutes.

Edward slept long and hard. The kind of sleep that leaves you groggy in the morning; wondering where exactly you were. His dreams that night were about pirates plundering ships and buried treasure. Common sense told him that pirates really didn't bury their treasure. They divided it up right away and usually spent it on wine and women. They didn't "bury it for a rainy day." A pirate's life expectancy in the 16th century was only a couple of years. They weren't thinking about putting money and treasures away for their later, golden years. But if that were true, what did he see last night in the cave beneath his house, Edward wondered as he continued to lay in bed.

The sun began to stream into the bedroom as it rose over the ocean, signaling that it was time to get up to start another day. Edward rubbed the sleep from his eyes, stretched, and sat up in bed very slowly. He tried to focus his thoughts before getting completely out of bed. As he did, he decided that, if nothing else, there were three things that he was going to accomplish on this day. Firstly, he was going to call off from work today. Being the boss afforded him the opportunity to come and go as he pleased. Plus, the magazine went to the printer yesterday. Not much to do until it returns and they have to distribute it.

Secondly, he was going to take a walk back down to the beach to see if he could unearth the entrance to the sand cave. Try to find any evidence of what he saw yesterday still existed. He had too many unanswered questions when it came to that cave and its contents. Thirdly, he was going to get Capt'n Petey out here to the beach for a couple of days. He wanted to take the captain out of Bath, out of his element, and onto Edward's home field to see if he could wear down the old sea captain and get more information from him that Edward was convinced he was still holding back.

Edward went into his home office, typed up an email to Char and Billy to let them know that he wouldn't be in today. He asked Char to call their temp workers to be ready to distribute the magazine to the various businesses and magazine boxes along the Outer Banks. The printer should have the copies available in the next couple of days. He also asked her to start printing labels for the subscriptions that will need to go out through the US mail. He then asked Billy to start working on the profile of local radio personality Chris Stephens. Chris had an interesting story to tell about losing his wife at a young age and moving back home with his 3 kids to the Outer Banks. He even wrote about it in a book titled "*Home Sweet Outer Banks Home?*" Should be a good human interest story Edward thought.

Once Edward hit send on the email to Char and Billy, he unplugged his cell phone from its charger and dialed the number for Capt'n Petey, hoping to catch him at home. As he had done the night before, Edward let the phone ring 10 times with no answer before hanging up. Getting worried Edward dialed the Old Country Kitchen.

On the third ring he heard, "Good morning Country Kitchen, this is Katie."

"Oh, hey Katie," Edward replied. "This is Edward Thatcher. Would Capt'n Petey be in for breakfast by any chance?"

“Hey, Mr Thatcher. Good to hear from you. I just want to say again that it was so nice of you to give Capt'n Petey a place to stay!”

“Thanks Katie. But it wasn't altogether entirely altruistic. I did need someone to watch over things. I mean, as was already proven, anyone could just break into a vacant house!” Edward laughed.

“Well, I guess you're right there Mr Thatcher. Stand by, the ol' captain, he is right here having breakfast this mornin'.”

Katie sat the phone down on the hostess station and called out to Capt'n Petey: “Hey Capt'n! Phone call for you!”

In the background Edward heard the captain complain about having to get up from his breakfast and letting it get cold. He also heard Katie admonish him by telling him to quit fussin' and to just answer the call.

“Yeah. This be Capt'n Petey. Who's makin' my breakfast get cold?”

“Hey Capt'n, this is Edward.”

“Oh, hey me boy. What be on yer mind this mornin'?”

“Captain, I'd like you to come out to the beach for a couple of days. I have something I want to show you. I also want to pick your brain a bit.”

“Pick me brain boy?”

“Yeah, Capt'n Petey,” Edward replied. “I'm working on this family mystery and I have something that you might be able to shed some light on. Plus I have an incredible story to tell you about last night.”

“Teach's Light get ya again, boy?” Captain Petey asked.

"Um, yeah. But how in the world...."

Interrupting Edward, Captain Petey responded, "Son, the ol' capt'n, he thinks maybe it be a good time for us to jaw a bit. Sounds like you might be ready at that."

"Great!" Edward exclaimed. "When is good for you to come to the beach?"

"Well my boy. The ol' capt'n, now he's got a captain's license, but no driving license. And I ain't got no car neither. Don't rightly know how I'm gonna make it to the Outer Banks."

Laughing, Edward replied, "No capt'n. I'll come get you and bring you back. And then bring you back to Bath again. It's not that far. Think I could come out this afternoon?"

"Boy, it be fine with the ol' capt'n, iffin' you want to come all the way back 'ere."

"Great Capt'n Petey!," Edward responded. "I'll be out this afternoon. Now go finish your breakfast before it gets cold!"

"Aye me boy. My thought too."

"See you later capt'n...."

Edward hung up the phone and went over to the Keurig to make his first cup of coffee of the day.

Taking his cup of hot coffee outside, Edward made his way to the deck on the Florida couple's house. He sat down and watched the ocean. About 50 yards off shore there were a flock of pelicans in the sky, trailing a pod of about 6 dolphin, swooping down and picking up the small fish that the dolphin left behind. Though he's experienced this scene hundreds of times since moving to the Outer Banks, it was one he never tired of.

Finishing off the coffee before it completely cooled off, Edward set his cup down on the bench and walked down to the beach. The sun was making its way to its zenith. The winds were gentle. A more perfect autumn day, you couldn't wish for. There were even a few families out on the beach on this day. A sight that hasn't been seen in several weeks due to the Nor'easter that blew through.

Edward traced his steps to the north. The same steps he made yesterday morning when he found the sand cave in the escarpment. Nothing. Same as last night. At this point the winds had smoothed everything over and there was not a single trace as to where the opening of the cave once was. Edward found it slightly amusing as he looked out at the dozen or so families stretched out on the sand, that they had no clue at all about them nearly sitting on a fortune of pirate treasure.

Edward walked the beach for a while that morning. After an hour or so, his stomach decided it was time to get something to eat. Not since Mama Kwans' fish tacos from the night before did he have anything. He figured on his way out of town to Bath to pick up the captain, he'd grab a crab meat omelet from Darrell's in Manteo.

Chapter 27

With a belly full of breakfast, Edward started for Bath. The day, being as picture perfect as it was, Edward decided to take the top off the Jeep and leave it behind at his house.

The 100 mile drive to his boyhood home on King Street took about 2 hours from the restaurant. Thankfully it was an uneventful drive. Edward, happy to see people back out on the roads and in the towns that dot the map between the Outer Banks and Bath. Edward pulled into the driveway just past noon. Finding the house locked, Edward used his key to let himself in. The captain wasn't home. Probably using the rest of that $128 he had left him on lunch Edward thought. Edward knew the captain did not have a cell phone so he grabbed an iced tea out of the refrigerator and sat down on the front porch to wait. The captain knew I'd be by this afternoon, he just didn't know when Edward reasoned.

As it turned out, Edward didn't have to wait all that long. After about 20 minutes or so, he noticed Captain Petey sauntering up King Street as he crossed over Carteret. Seeing Edward sitting on the porch, the Captain yelled out a hello.

"And hello to you Capt'n Petey," Edward replied back.

"Didn't know rightly when to expect you sonny. But 'afore we left, I wanted to run down to tend to your folks graves. Make it all pretty and such. Told ya, I'd take care of them all nice."

Turning away from the crusty ol' sea captain so he wouldn't see Edward wipe a tear from his eye, he replied back to Petey, "Thank you captain. My mother and father, they deserve to have a nice place to rest. I appreciate you taking care of them."

"Me boy. It be a real honor fer me to take care of them. Your maw and paw were good folks. I expect ain't many like them in this big ol' world of ours."

“I expect you are right Petey.” Edward replied. “Why don't you go in and gather some things for the trip. I want to go out and see my parents for a couple of minutes before we leave.”

“Aye me boy. Glad you do that. It be the right thing to do.”

Captain Petey went into the house to pack his things. Not that he had all that much to pack. One extra pair of pants and a shirt with some underwear and socks. The captain also grabbed a toothbrush and threw the items into a plastic to go bag from the Old Country Kitchen.

Edward slid behind the wheel of the Jeep and drove the quarter mile or so to the St Thomas Episcopal Church Cemetery where his parents lay. He stepped from the car and walked the few yards to their plot. Edward stood there for a few moments without saying or thinking anything.

Finally, softly, shaky, Edward said “Hey mom. Hey pop. Its me, Edward. But I guess you already know that looking down on me from heaven and all.”

Taking a deep breath, Edward continued, “Well, I've been working on what you've wanted to tell me all these years. Along the way I've figured out that Capt'n Petey was your brother, dad. I've got him living at the house taking care of things for me He's taking care of you and ma too He's got these pretty flowers planted here.” Edward took a deep breath and continued, “Some strange stuff has been happening pops. I found what appears to be Blackbeard's treasure and what looks like an old family Bible. Weird, the handwriting in the Bible is a lot like yours pop. My guess is that the family Bible belonged to the pirate himself. Anyway, I'm going to take Petey back to Nags Head with me. Show him the book. See if he can shed any light on it.”

Edward bent down and picked a weed from next to one of the flowers before continuing. “Well that’s it mom and dad. Don’t know what else to say. I’ll do my best to get back here as often as I can to see you and to visit with my new found uncle. I just hope that I’m on the right path with all of this.”

With that, a gentle breeze rustled the leaves of the massive oak that hung over his parents grave site. Edward took that to be a message from his parents that yes, he was on the right track and to keep going. Edward did a sign of the cross, wiped another tear from his eye and got back in the Jeep to collect Capt’n Petey and start the drive back to the Outer Banks.

On the way back to Nags Head, there wasn’t much conversation between Capt’n Petey and Edward. Not having the top on the Jeep likely played a role in that, being too loud really to have a conversation without shouting.

Once they crossed the Pungo River, Edward turned the Jeep into the Speedway gas station to fill the tank. With the Jeep’s gas tank was topped off, Edward ran inside to grab a couple of coffees. One for him and one for Captain Petey. He got back behind the wheel and pointed the Jeep back toward home at the beach.

Once they got to the Virginia Dare Memorial Bridge to cross the Croatan Sound, Edward looked to his right and yelled to Petey, “You hungry? Want to stop for an early dinner?”

Shouting back over the rush of the wind, Captain Petey replied “I could eat boy. Ain't had nothin’ since breakfast. And that was just oatmeal. Damn doctor! I swear, he be tryin’ to kill the ol’ capt’n with that dang oatmeal e’ry danged day!”

“Good! I know just the place. I feel like some fried oysters and a cold blonde myself!”

“Boy, wait. Yer fixin’to git you’self a girl?”

Laughing, Edward replied “No capt’n. A blonde is Kitty Hawk Blonde Ale put out by the local Lost Colony Brewery.”

“Oh. Yep, the ol’ capt’n, he could go fer a cold one his’self.”

Getting to the end of the bridge and to the junction of Manteo and Wanchese, Edward turned left onto Route 64. Just past Darrell’s, where Edward had breakfast earlier today, he turned right into the Shallowbag Bay Club and parked right outside the front door of Striper’s Bar & Grill.

The two men, uncle and nephew, climbed out of the Jeep and went into the restaurant. Edward asked for a table for two outside. Because it was only 3 in the afternoon, and the dinner rush had not yet started, they were able to get a table immediately. Once settled in, a server, a young girl who introduced herself as Bobbie came by to take the drink order.

“What do you say capt’n? Want to try a blonde?”

Looking a bit embarrassed by how the question was phrased in front of a young lady, Capt’n Petey replied, “Sure. I’ll take me one of those beers.”

“Bobbie, The Captain and I will have two Kitty Hawk Blondes please.”

“Yes sir,” Bobbie replied. “Frosted glasses with those beers?”

“Sure. Thanks Bobbie.” Edward replied.

While looking over the menu, it was Captain Petey that spoke first. “Ooh Wee, them prices be high me boy. You sure you about eatin’ here?”

“Its fine Petey. This is a great place. Just order anything you want,” Edward said reassuring the captain. “I think I’ll have the fried oysters with the fries and cole slaw. Probably have a second blonde too.” Edward specifically said it just like that, knowing it made the captain a little embarrassed.

"Well, my boy, reckon iffin' you don't care none, the ol' captain, he's got a hankerin' for the shrimp & grits. But I'll git the lil' size so it not cost so much money fer ya."

Bobbie had just returned to the table, poured each beer into the frosted mugs and asked, "you fellas ready to order?"

"I expect we are," Edward replied. "I'll have the fried oysters with fries and cole slaw."

"Very good sir," Bobbie replied. Now turning her attention to Capt'n Petey, she said "….and you sir?"

"Reckon I'll do the shrimp and grits. But make it 'da small one. Too much money fer a big!"

Edward interjected, "Bobbie, don't listen to him. He'll take the large portion of the shrimp and grits."

Looking over to the captain Bobbie said, "that ok with you sir?"

"Reckon you do what the boy says to do ma'am." Captain Petey replied. "He be 'da boss."

"Very good sirs. I'll get your order in right away for you. Pretty day to be sittin' outside," Bobbie said as she looked briefly at the water of Shallowbag Bay before going back inside to place their order.

Picking up his beer from the table and taking a couple of large gulps, the captain looked at Edward and said, "Well boy. We drove all this way without jawin' at all. You wanna tell the ol' capt'n what it was you saw last night and what it is you want to show 'im?"

Edward also picked up his beer and took a couple of sips, he looked at the other diners at the adjacent tables before replying. "Well, Petey, to tell you the truth I don't think we should talk about it here. Out in the open like this. I think we should wait till we get home."

"Suit yerself me boy," Capt'n Petey said as he took another sip of his Kitty Hawk Blonde Ale.

It was just a few moments later when Bobbie brought the meals to the table. Both Edward and the captain ordered another round of beers. The conversation during the meal was mundane. Things like the weather, the magazine, Capt'n Petey's fishing experiences. Both doing the best they could to steer away from the conversation that seemed to be the white elephant in the room.

It was a half hour later, when the dinners were finished, the beers drained and the check paid. Edward and the captain climbed back into the Jeep and made the 20 minute ride back to Edward's beach box in Nags Head.

Turning into the driveway Edward leaned over to the captain and said, "Well, here we are capt'n, the palatial Thatcher estate."

"Don't rightly know what palatial means, me boy," the captain replied. "But yer home, it sure looks.....a bit cozy."

Laughing, Edward replied, "yeah, reckon cozy is a word to describe it."

The two men went inside, Edward leading Capt'n Petey to the bedroom.

"You stay here capt'n. I'll stay on the futon in my office."

"Me lad, you don't need to put yerself out none. The ol' captain, he's slept on rocking boats in the middle of the ocean and on floors in shacks on land. I don't need no fancy bed.

Hearing nothing of it, Edward waved off his protest and said, "Capt'n, I insist. You're my guest and I want you to be comfortable."

And for the second time in about an hour the captain replied with “Suit yerself boy.”

Once all of Captain Petey’s gear was stowed, Edward took the captain out to the porch on the Florida couple’s home.

“Well, capt’n, you asked why you were here. This is why.”

“Well, boy, it be a might pretty here, but this ain’t why you brung me here, to look at water, sand, and pretty girls.”

“No, capt’n, you’re right about that. I want to tell you what happened to me the other day here.”

“Go on boy,” The captain replied. The way Capt’n Petey replied, the inflection in his voice, made Edward think to himself that Captain Petey already knew what he was going to say.

“Ok capt’n. I don’t rightly know where to start.....”

“At the beginning is a good place I’d always hear,” the captain interjected.

“Yeah, reckon you’re right,” Edward said. “Well, the storm that we’ve been having both here and in Bath....”

“Yup, nasty Nor’easter. Ain’t hardly never seen one like that ‘afore”

“Yeah,” Edward continued. “Well, the storm, it well, it created this huge cliff in this dune that we’re sitting behind. The wind kept hammering it and hammering it, and before too long it had revealed an opening into a cave that lays beneath it.”

“Aye, me boy. And you went explorin’ I’ll bet.

“Not sure if exploring is the right word exactly. At first I just kind of poked my head into it, but it was comin’ up on high tide and thought it better that I get out out of there.”

"Aye, sounds like the smart thing to do my laddie."

"Yeah. I got myself off the beach and back home. Then a couple of nights ago, about 2:30 in the morning or so, that bright light was back."

"Aye boy, Ol' Teach's Light I expect."

"I'm beginning to think it was now too capt'n. Anyway, it was back and I went chasing it out to the beach. But as I got to this point right where we are sitting, POOF, it was gone. Just disappeared!"

"What you do then boy?"

"Not much I could do. I went back home and went to bed. But I couldn't sleep. Too much running through my mind, so when the sun came up I came back out here to investigate further."

"…and what didja find me boy?" The captain asked.

"Let's take a walk Capt'n Petey, and I'll show you. Well, sort of."

The two men left the porch and made their way down to the beach. Edward walked a bit north and stopped.

"Why you stop 'ere boy?"

"It was right about here capt'n."

"What was here?"

"That's the next part of the story. It was right about here where the entrance to the sand cave was."

"Don't look like no cave 'ere boy. Ya sure?"

"Yes. Well, no. Not sure this is exactly where it was. But it was around this area somewhere."

“Ya go in laddie?”

“I did. And for the last part of the story, let’s go back to the house. There’s something there to show you.”

“"Tis yer story boy.”

The two walked back to Edward’s house. The captain and Edward had a seat in the small living room before Edward picked up the story. He told the captain about the corridor to the right of the cave entrance. He told the captain of the light shining from deep inside the corridor. He told the captain about the large room where he found the light hovering. And he told the captain about the pirate treasure spilling out of an old pirate’s chest. The coins, the jewels, the gold crowns. And Edward told the captain that he found one other item. And for that he excused himself and went into his office.

A second later Edward came out holding the white Bible that he retrieved from the sand cave, “Take a look at this capt’n.” Edward said as he handed the book to Capt’n Petey. “This is what I took out of the cave with me. It looks like a Bible of some sort. But I’m confused why a pirate captain would have a family Bible. It seems to me pirates always aligned themselves with the devil.”

Carefully leafing through the ancient book, the captain was silent for a long while. Finally he said “It do look like a family Bible fer sure. This all you took out the cave sonny?”

“Yeah capt’n Petey. It was weird too.”

“How’s that boy?”

“Well, the light....”

“That be Capt’n Teach watchin’ over his treasure, I’d expect.”

"Maybe Capt'n Petey. Maybe. But anyway, the light.....it seemed like it wanted me to take the book with me. I can't rightly explain how, but when I leaned down to get it and look at it, the light, well it didn't waver or stop me."

"Reckon ol' Teach wanted you to have it me boy."

"But why do you think that might be Capt'n?"

"Reckon, you'll figure that out laddie."

Edward, still convinced that Captain Petey knew more than he was saying stopped talking for a few minutes while the captain leafed through the pages of the "Blackbeard Bible." Once the silence became a bit awkward, Edward finally said, "look at the inside back cover capt'n."

Flipping carefully to the spot that Edward instructed, the captain sat there for a long time looking. Not saying anything, just looking. Finally Captain Petey responded, "sure looks like yer paw's writin', don't it?"

"See, that what I thought too Capt'n Petey. It sure does look like pops. Can't really make out what it says though..."

"Yeah, it be a bit faded fer sure. It looks to the ol' capt'n to be a chart. Not a nautical chart, but a writin' chart."

"Not like a buried treasure chart though. I mean, why would there be a chart for the buried treasure, when the book was buried *with* the buried treasure?"

"No me boy. This look like it be a list of names."

"Maybe a listing of the pirates on his ship," Edward offered up as explanation.

"Don't reckon so," Captain Petey answered. "Not enough names 'ere to round out a boat of blood-thirsty cutthroats."

"Reckon you're right about that capt'n."

"When the ol' capt'n has a problem to solve, reckon the best thing is to not think about it. The ol' capt'n, he waits fer the answer to come to 'im. Usually does at some point."

With that Captain Petey carefully closed the book and handed it back to Edward.

"Boy, what I can tell you, is you sure be onto somethin' 'ere. Don't give up on it."

Still not convinced the captain was telling all that he knew, Edward took the Bible from him, walked back into the office and carefully placed it back in the desk drawer.

The sun was starting to set now on the Outer Banks. Edward suggested to the captain that they walk across the street to the Lucky 12 Tavern to have a night cap. Captain readily agreed with one condition. "I still gots me some of that money you gave da ol' captain. I'm buyin' tonight."

"Yes sir capt'n." Edward said. And knowing that the reference made Captain Petey a bit unsettled, Edward said further "tonight the blondes are on you!"

"Aye me boy, the blondes are on me...."

Chapter 28

The two men walked across the street to the Lucky 12. They perched themselves on the high top round table in front of the room that contained the pool table. The conversation stayed away from pirates and bibles and buried treasure. Mostly the men talked about their upbringing. Captain Petey of course knew most of Edward's life, having played many hours of checkers and spent many hours of watching baseball with Edward Senior.

Edward however was delighted to learn more of the life of Capt'n Peter E Dussault. How as a young boy, spent time in an orphanage before being adopted by the Dussault couple, Charlie and Miriam. The Dussaults had tried for years to have a baby without any luck. Modern science wasn't so modern back then, so they went the adoption route. Charlie wanted a son. Someone who could take over the family fishing boat when Charlie would finally retire. Captain Petey didn't have much in the way of formal schooling since he was always helping out Charlie on the boat. A fisherman's life is not an easy one. If you didn't catch fish, you didn't eat. Life was black and white like that. Especially back then.

"Then pert near 5, 6 years ago, I reckon,"Captain Petey said to Edward, "it was your maw that found out me and yer paw be brothers. The ol' capt'n, he don't know how she found out. Not sure yer paw ever did neither. It was right after that Pam died. Sad day fer yer paw. I don't know he ever rightly got over it."

Waves of guilt again started filling Edward. "I shoulda been there more," Edward said softly to himself.

Captain Petey heard him and chose to ignore it.

Edward asked, "What ever happened to the family fishing boat? I mean, you told me you were fishing with someone else the first time you saw Teach's Light."

"Aye laddie, that be true. It be sad. Like I told ya'. Back then if ya didn't catch fish ya didn't eat."

"I remember."

"Well, my paw. He had a rough spot. Not catchin' much. He went out each day. Most days I went wit 'im, but we'd come home wit nothin'. Just an empty tank of fuel. Nothin' else."

"Must have been tough," Edward interjected.

"Aye me boy. It 'twas. And my paw, he felt mighty low 'bout it. One mornin' he got up and took the boat out. 'Member, we didn't have no fancy weather radar like they gots now. He knowed the water be rough that day. The winds be buildin' out of the northeast. But he figured we has to eat. So, he tries to git some fish. He didn't let me help this time. He said it be too rough. Well, me boy, he went out to catch some food for me and my maw...."

Captain Petey stopped for a second, seemingly trying to compose himself before continuing, Edward thought.

"Welp, like the ol' capt'n said, it be a blow, and that be the last time my maw and me ever see'd my paw. No one ever found him or the boat."

"Captain Petey, I'm so sorry. That must have been an awful time for you."

"It was me boy. Hard on my maw mostly. There was some wreckage found 'bout a month later. The sheriff, he said it be from my paw's boat."

"Was it?" Edward asked.

"Don't rightly know laddie. Didn't make no difference neither. I be like 14, 15 at the time. No more time for school for me. I had to hire out on other boats to help feed me and my maw."

“Wow Capt’n. You didn’t have an easy go of it.”

“It be fine sonny. The ol’ capt’n, he took care of his’self. But sure felt badly for my maw. My maw died right after paw went missin’. They said she died of a broken heart. Don’t rightly know if that’s a thing, but it surely made sense. Been on me own ever since.”

The two men sat there in silence for a while after that. They finished their beers and ordered a second round. Deciding to take some of the heaviness out of the evening, Edward suggested the two men play a round of 8 ball.

“Boy, I’d play you, but I’d play in pool halls ‘round the world. Reckon, you best be ready to lose...”

Racking up the balls Edward said “Give it your best shot old man....”

Edward and Captain Petey played 3 games of 8 ball. Petey wasn’t lying, he surely knew how to play. In fact he won 2 of the 3 games. When they were done, they put the pool cues back in the rack. Captain Petey, true to his word, pulled the crumpled bills that Edward had given him out of his left front pocket and paid the bill for the 4 beers.

Then the two men, feeling closer than they had just a couple of hours before, walked back across the street to Edward’s house to retire for the evening. It had been a long day and both men were tired, both physically and mentally.

Chapter 29

Captain Petey retired to his bedroom. Edward to his on the futon in the office. Of course with all of the questions still swirling around in Edward's head, he pulled the Bible back out and leafed through it. He tried to make out the handwriting on the back inside cover. After a considerable amount of time, he thought he finally made out the faded words:

Edward "Ned" Teach (38) marryed Mary Ormond (16) - 1718.
1 son, Edward II, little Ned.

Married, spelled in the Old English of the day.

Edward closed the book, pleased that he was able to finally put some answers to the questions. This was in fact, the family Bible of Edward Teach, the notorious Blackbeard the Pirate. And if Edward was right, the old pirate captain wanted him to have the book. For what, he still didn't know.

In his bedroom, Captain Petey was also having a bit of trouble falling asleep. Used to being rocked to sleep by the waves of the waters on which he fished, the captain often didn't sleep well on land.

Captain Petey laid awake in bed thinking about the story that Edward had just told him that night. The sand cave. The buried treasure. Ol' Teach watching over it, along with the Bible. Capt'n Teach allowing the book to leave. Captain Petey thought about the writing and how similar it was to his own brother. A brother that he didn't even know he had until fairly recently. He knew that Edward, the young man in the other room that turned out to be his nephew, thought he knew more about the family than he has already said. Perhaps that was true. But he wasn't so sure himself. Yes, he had some answers, but he also had some gaps that didn't seem to all fit snugly together.

After a while, Capt'n Petey got up out of bed. He didn't want to disturb Edward so he stayed in his room. He opened the closet in the bedroom. He wasn't sure why. He felt like he was directed to do it. A whole lot lately hadn't been making a whole lot of sense to him. But he just went with the flow.

In the back of the closet, there was a big steamer trunk off to the right. From underneath it, Capt'n Petey noticed what looked like a missing piece of the floor. Already feeling a bit weird about invading Edward's privacy, the captain didn't pry any further. Instead he went back to his bed, laid down and eventually drifted off to sleep.

Chapter 30

Both Edward and Captain Petey were up with the sun.

While turning on the coffee maker, Edward asked the captain how he slept.

“Just fair, me boy. I ain’t never been the one to sleep on dry land. Plus, ya given this ol’ captain a right many things to think on.”

“Yes sir, Capt’n.” Edward replied. “Got some more for you too.”

“How’s that me laddie?”

“Well, last night, I couldn’t sleep right away. Had too many things runnin’ around my brain. Anyway, I pulled the Bible back out, and after some real serious studying, I think I made something out of the handwriting in the back.” Edward handed the book to the capt’n and showed him what he thought it said.

“You might be on to somethin’ there sonny.” The Captain replied. “Iffin’ I squint just right, I sees what you seein’.”

Edward took the book back from Petey and put it back in the desk drawer. He went over to the Keurig and dropped a pod of Cafe Bustelo in it and hit brew. A few seconds later, he took the cup and handed it to the captain. He then went over and dropped in a pod for himself.

“Capt’n, I’ll be honest. I don’t know what to do with that information, or where to go with it.”

Captain Petey took a slow, careful sip from his hot coffee, while Edward grabbed his from the coffee maker. He set the cup down on the kitchen table and said, “Sonny, I don’t want ya to thunk the ol’ sea capt’n here was nosy or nothin.’ But I went in yer closet last night ‘cause I couldn’t sleep. I saw yer steamer trunk in there.”

"Yeah, not really anything of note in there Capt'n. Just some old papers. Some old clothes that don't fit anymore." Edward replied, a little annoyed that Petey seemed to be rifling through his personal belongings.

"'T'weren't the trunk the ol' capt'n found intrestin'."

"No? What then was interesting?" Edward asked.

"Well, again, the ol' capt'n, he weren't snoopin' or nothin.' But I saw a missin' piece o' floor 'neath that big trunk."

Edward thought back. He remembered now that when he put that trunk in there, he did cover up a piece of missing floor. At the time he had made a mental note to fix it, but as time went by, and with that steamer trunk hiding it, Edward had completely forgotten about it. "Reckon I forgot to fix that," he replied.

"Might be nothin'. Don't know fer sure. Might be somethin'. Don't know that fer sure neither. But you, me boy, you said that Teach's ol' treasure is right 'cheer underneath the house."

Edward, not having put two and two together on that till just now took a sip of his black coffee, set it back down and stared off a bit into space. The captain let him just think about it for a while. Both men sipping their coffee in silence.

Finally Edward said, "you know captain. I think it's a long shot, but I think we should take that steamer trunk out of the closet and investigate it a little more. What do you think?"

"Not a bad plan me boy, 'iffin that's what you want to do."

The two men went back into Edward's bedroom. With some difficulty, they pulled the trunk out of the closet and hoisted it up onto the bed. Edward got down on his hands and knees and looked at the space in the floor missing a plank of wood. He couldn't see anything. He went into the laundry room where he kept his tool box and came back with a hammer and a small pry bar. He carefully went to the piece of wood next to the empty space and pried that from the floor, not wanting to damage it, so it could be hammered back into place later. There still wasn't much to see, so Edward pried the next piece loose. Then the next. And the next. Soon Edward had 8 pieces of floor planking stacked in his bedroom. He shined a flash light into the newly formed hole in the bedroom closet. First he shined it to the left. And then to the right. On the far right side of the hole, right in the very corner, Edward noticed something. He couldn't quite tell what it was, but it wasn't the sandy ground that was beneath the rest of the removed flooring. Edward moved further into the closet prying up more pieces of the closet floor, handing them to Captain Petey, who stacked them in the corner.

"See anythin' yet me boy?"

"Something Petey. Just not sure what yet. I think we'll know more with a couple more of these floor pieces gone." With that, he handed another piece to Capt'n Petey to stack with the others.

It couldn't have been more than 3 minutes and 2 floor board pieces later when the capt'n heard Edward exclaim, "Well, I'll be a son-of-a-bitch!"

"What boy? What ya seein' in there?"

"Captain, I don't know if you'd believe me. You best come see for yourself."

Edward moved off to the one side of the closet to allow Capt'n Petey to get on his hands and knees to look into the newly formed hole in the floor. Shining the flash light in, it was Petey's turn to exclaim, "Boy! That's it! I knowed we'd figure this out!"

Chapter 31

Edward and Captain Petey removed enough of the floorboards to see the trap door that laid beneath the closet floor. Edward reached down and was not able to move the door. It wasn't locked! But the space was also not large enough for either man to climb down to it. So Edward and the capt'n spent the better part of the next hour painstakingly pulling up the rest of the closet flooring. Finally, Edward was able to reach down to the trap door handle and pull.

And he pulled.

And he pulled.

The trap door wouldn't open. It wasn't locked. It just wouldn't open.

"See there my laddie." The capt'n finally said. "Those latches. They look rusty and froze in place."

"Yeah, I see that now Capt'n Petey," Edward replied.

"Not never gonna git that door opened just a heavin' on it. Looks to the ol' capt'n like it ain't been open fer a good long while."

Sitting on the sand floor in what used to be his closet, Edward sat back and thought about it a moment. "Got to be someway to un-seize that metal." For all the smarts Edward had about putting a magazine out, he sure wasn't the handiest guy in town.

A second or two later, Edward sprung to his feet and went into the laundry room to his toolbox once again. After shuffling through the items in the box, he finally came up with what he was looking for. A can of WD 40, though it was close to being empty.

Edward took it back to the closet and sprayed the hinges on the trap door. Just a few seconds later the can just blew air. The un-seizing spray was empty. Edward tugged at the door a few more times, but it was still stuck.

"Now what laddie?" The captain asked.

"Don't know for sure Petey. Reckon I've got a friend or two that might be able to use a torch to cut this open."

"Don't reckon we should do that sonny. Don't want too many people to knowed what we're doin' in 'ere. 'Specially iffin' we thinks we knowed what might be in there."

"Yeah, you're right Capt'n Petey. Right now no one except me and you should know what's going on here."

Edward thought maybe a new can of WD 40 might be what they should try next. In all honesty, the amount that was in the old can probably wasn't enough to really have done any good. So Edward climbed back out of the hole, dusted himself off, grabbed his keys and he and Captain Petey made a run to Lowes, up on the ByPass in Kill Devil Hills.

For the first part of the drive, neither man said much of anything, but it was Capt'n Petey that finally broke the silence. "So me boy, I was thinkin'...."

"Yeah, capt'n. Me too. But you go first."

"Supposin' jest fer a second, supposin' what we find down in that hole is the room you was in. And supposin' we find the treasure of ol' Captain Teach. Then what?"

"I don't know capt'n. On one hand, we wouldn't have to ever worry about money again. You and me, we'd be richer than we ever thought we could be. But then again, is it the right thing to do? Maybe we should just let it rest there and not bother it."

"Me boy, the ol' capt'n, he sure 'nuff glad to heard ya say that. Me thinks it be bad luck to move it."

Not believing much in superstition, Edward wasn't sure how to reply. He did think, however, that just a few short weeks ago he didn't believe in Teach's Light either, but now well.....

"You might be right about that Capt'n Petey. But first, let's just see what's down there before we decide anything. Might just be a wild goose chase after all." Edward said as he turned the Jeep into the parking lot of the Lowes Home Improvement store.

While walking the aisles looking for the WD 40, Edward also figured he'd pick up a larger pry bar. One bigger than he had when lifting the floorboards of the closet. He also picked up a box of flooring nails so that he could also put the floor back into place once their investigation was complete.

Fifteen minutes later, Edward and Captain Petey were on their way back home with their supplies.

Edward climbed down into the hole of the closet floor and emptied the entire can of WD 40 onto the latches of the door. He decided to let it set and work itself in before attempting to open the door again.

"Let's let that stuff penetrate the latches for a few minutes. Let it get to working." Edward said as he pulled himself back up and into the house.

"Whatever you thinks my boy," the captain replied. "Sure could use 'nother cup of that coffee whilst we wait. Sure is the best this ol' capt'n ever tasted 'afore."

The two men went into the kitchen where Edward made them two cups of the Cafe Bustelo. They sat there silently drinking from their cups. Finally Edward sat his empty cup back down and said, "Well capt'n. Let's give it another try. Let's see if that stuff worked on those latches."

“Right behind you me boy.” The captain replied.

Edward climbed back down. He pulled at the door. There was more play in it now than there had been before. The captain, laying on his belly in the bedroom above, lent a hand and both men heaved. The door was moving, just not enough to open.

They rested a second, and once again in combined forces they pulled at the door. Capt'n Petey using the large pry bar to loosen the door around the frame.

The door creaked. It groaned. It put up a hell of a fight, and then finally, it swung open!

Edward and Captain Petey looked through the door, with the aid of the flash light app on Edward’s phone, and were crestfallen at what they saw next…..

Chapter 32

There beneath the trap door that they struggled to gain access to, for the better part of several hours, laid......another trap door.

The sight of another door, took the wind out of the sails of both men. Realizing that they haven't had breakfast yet as it was approaching the lunch hour, it was Edward that proposed the two men take a break and run to grab something to eat. The captain readily agreed.

Wanting to grab something quick, Edward drove them to the Outer Banks Mall and pulled into a parking spot right in front of the doors at the Grits Grill. Edward and Captain Petey took two seats at the counter and each ordered the biscuits and gravy and coffee.

“Sure ‘nough not as good as yer coffee” Capt'n Petey said as he took his first sip.

“No, but I reckon it's hot.” Edward replied.

Edward and the capt'n, on the drive over, decided that they would not discuss in public what they were working on back home in the bedroom closet. Never can tell what sort of prying ears may be listening in. But with dreams of wild riches racing through their heads, the two men had a tough time thinking of anything else. So they said very little to each other as the breakfast was served. Mainly just staring blankly at the tv screen in the restaurant that was playing CNN News.

Soon enough, both Edward and the captain finished up their meals and were on their way back home to their next project. The second trap door.

Edward and Capt'n Petey went back into the bedroom. Edward particularly not looking forward to trying to figure out how to open this second door. But it turned out that all his fear was for naught. He gave three pull tugs on the handle, and immediately this one opened right up…

As soon as the door was completely opened, both Edward and Capt'n Petey saw it. It was a tunnel, similar to the one Edward had walked through from the beach side cave. The other thing they saw was a light, that illuminated from deep within the tunnel.

"Well capt'n, we're at the point of no return I expect." Edward said.

"I expect ya right, me laddie." The captain replied.

The tunnel wasn't wide enough for both Edward and Captain Petey to walk side by side. One had to follow the other. Not wanting to show any fear, it was Edward that took the point.

There were some twists and turns in the tunnel. Bending to the right and then back to the left. As was the case with the tunnel from the beach, this one also had a slight downward angle to it, as they went deeper and deeper into the sand above them. With each step, the light shone brighter and brighter.

The two men walked, what seemed close to a quarter mile, when Edward stopped. "What do you think Capt'n Petey? Should we continue on? It might be dangerous up ahead. Especially if that is Blackbeard's ghost guarding his treasure."

"I expect it be Ol' Captain Teach alright. But, I have a feelin' we'd be safe 'nuff."

"How can you know that?" Edward asked.

"Boy, 'member when the ol' capt'n told ya that me and yer paw talked 'afore he died?"

"Yeah, capt'n, so?"

"'Member I said there were things you can't know yet. You had to figure 'dose things out yerself?"

"Yeah.....is this part of figuring it out capt'n?"

"Reckon so my boy. You keep walkin', this here ol' capt'n, he expect everything be ok."

Edward, not sure what to make of what Captain Petey just said, but trusted him as he moved forward at a slower pace than he had before.

Two more twists in the tunnel and Edward and Captain Petey found themselves at the opposite end of the large room that Edward had found himself in before. In the center again was the large treasure chest spilling over with the same jewels, gold crowns and Spanish Doubloons.

The light hovering above it all glowing brightly. It didn't move. It just hovered in mid-air. Edward stopped and just stood. He didn't know what to do next.

It was Captain Petey that spoke first. And he spoke directly to the light. "Ol' Captain Teach. 'Dis here be Capt'n Petey Dussault. I be born originally as a Thatcher, just like my friend Edward here. He be the son of Edward Drummond Thatcher Senior from Bath, North Carolina. I be Edward Senior's brother."

Edward shifted his sight from the light to Capt'n Petey and back to the light, not saying a word.

Captain Petey continued, "My brother, he told me the story right after, this here boy's maw died. He told me alright. And this boy, right here. He told me he be here 'afore and that you let 'im take the Bible outta here. Reckon you knowed who he be, didn't cha?

Petey stopped talking and waited to see if the light hovering above the room would reply back.

After a few minutes of silence, Capt'n Petey yelled out, "Whatsa 'matta you ol' buzzard? I knowed ya can talk. My brother telled me!"

Captain Petey remained silent again for several seconds.

Then the room started to vibrate. The light grew brighter. And a voice that seemed to bellow from deep within the cave itself bellowed out, like the wizard in the Wizard of Oz.

"Who dares to disturb the treasure of Captain Ned Teach?"

Edward had to grab a hold of himself to keep from running back through the tunnel and into the safety of his house.

Again, the room started to vibrate and the light grew brighter. So bright now that Edward and Captain Petey had to shade their eyes from it. And again the voice wanted to know, this time yelling it out:

'WHO DARES TO DISTURB THE TREASURE OF CAPTAIN NED TEACH?"

Captain Petey, rising to his full 5 foot 9 inch frame answered back, "I done already told ya. We be the brother and the son of Edward Drummond Thatcher Senior of Bath, North Carolina. Now is 'dis how ya treat kin?"

"Kin? What do you mean kin?" Edward shrieked.

"Me boy, it be the part you been waitin' on. The part I knowed from yer paw. See, Ol' Captain Teach here, he married Mary Ormond when he be 38 and she be 16 back in da 1700's."

"1718 to be exact." Edward replied.

"Yeah, 1718. They had 'dem a boy. Lil' Neddie is what Mary called 'im, after his paw."

"Right. I read that Capt'n but could never find out what ever happened to him." Edward responded.

"Well, the history books, they don't talk about Lil' Neddie. He be born after Ol' Captain Teach here got hisself kilt by that Maynard feller. Mary, she don't want people to think poorly of Lil' Neddie 'cause of what his paw was. So she called 'im Neddie and changed their last name from Teach to Thatcher. Same name as you and me boy."

Captain Petey stopped talking and looked at the light, waiting to see if Captain Teach might jump in. When Capt'n Petey realized he wasn't, Captain Petey continued. "Now, ol' Capt'n Teach 'ere. He have 'dis light he comes back as. He been hoverin' in Bath and in Ocracoke where he was kilt. They say he watchin' over his treasure. And I expect he is. At some point when his wife Mary died, ol Capt'n Teach here, musta found that Bible you have up at the house. He musta found it and brought it back here to where nobody else can find it. He didn't want nobody to pester his family, most of which his boy Lil' Neddie, just 'cause they have the same blood in their veins as the pirate captain. Didn't want no evidence to be found."

Captain Petey stopped and looked at the bright light and said, "How my doin' Capt'n Teach? Sound 'bout right to you?"

Both Captain Petey and Edward looked at the light. It glowed brighter as the sound started to reverberate from deep within it. "Aye. You be the blood of Captain Ned Teach, known throughout the world as the mighty Blackbeard the Pirate!"

Mustering up enough courage to speak, Edward asked, "So Capt'n Petey, this is what you've known all along but didn't think I could know it right away?"

“Aye, laddie. Yer paw, he wanted you to know ‘bout the family. But he also thinked it best fer you to figure some things out fer yerself.”

The light started glowing brighter again as the voice of the Blackbeard ghost proclaimed, “You be the blood alright, but this be the treasure of Captain Ned Teach. Go from here and never return. The treasure must never be disturbed or the curse of Blackbeard will come down upon you, kin or not! Now LEAVE THIS PLACE!!!”

Edward and Captain Petey wasted no time running from the large room. As they did they heard a large crash. Looking back Edward saw the large room in the cave come tumbling down. Gone, as though it never existed. The two men ran as fast as they could, the corridors behind them filling with sand as they finally made their way back up the twists and turns of the tunnel to the first of the trap doors. They scampered through it and closed the door behind them. Opened the last of the two doors, jumped through that and also closed it. They sat on the floor of the bedroom breathing heavily, trying to catch their breath.

“Well, me boy,” Capt’n Petey said. “Looks like ya got yer answer ‘bout that treasure. It’s got to stay where it be boy. No sense riling the ghost of ol’ Ned Teach.”

“I think you are right about that Captain Petey. I think Captain Teach will have to spend all of eternity guarding those riches. His price to pay for having spent his life as a cutthroat pirate.”

“Aye, me laddie. Hard way to go through the rest of time.” Captain Petey replied.

Edward and Captain Petey spent the next several hours nailing back down the flooring in the bedroom closet, still leaving the one piece of board that was missing. They slid the steamer trunk back over it as Edward made a mental note to once again replace the missing piece in the near future, as he did once before.

Chapter 33

Edward and Captain Petey spent a couple more days together before Edward was to drive Capt'n Petey, his newly found uncle, back to the family home on King Street in Bath. Capt'n Petey filled Edward in on stories of Edward's maw and paw and how his paw took it so hard when Pam died. He told Edward about the times that Captain Petey and Edward Senior spent together. The conversations they had. One conversation Edward found particularly interesting.

"Petey, when we were walking through the tunnel, how did you know it would be be safe to continue on into the room?"

"Well, me boy, ain't da first time a Thatcher be in that room." Captain Petey explained.

"You mean you've been in there before?"

"Not me, my boy." Petey replied. "Reckon it be yer paw that was."

"When was that?"

"Yer paw, when he heard you was movin' to the beach fer good, he and yer maw, figured they'd come over to this house and git it ready for you to live in it."

"Yeah, I remember telling them not to fuss about it."

"Well 'dey did laddie. Yer maw, she wanted to git it clean and yer paw, he wanted to do some paintin' and repairs. It was yer maw that found the hole in the closet floor when she be sweepin'. She told yer paw to put in a whole new floor 'afore you moved in."

"So mom was the one who found the trap door originally?"

"Reckon she was me boy." Petey answered. "Yer paw, he told me that he went out to Griggs Lumber to git some new boards when yer maw pulled the old ones out. Just 'afore yer paw got back, yer maw, she found the trap door."

"How did she open it by herself?" Edward wanted to know.

"She didn't boy. She waited 'till yer paw got back and they opened it together."

"And they went down?"

"They did me boy. They saw the light, just like you and me did. They followed that tunnel all the way to the back into that big room."

"And they saw Captain Teach too?"

"Aye boy, indeed they did. They saw all the treasure. And they talked to ol' Ned. They also seen that ol' Bible, but left it down there."

"Do you know what Captain Teach said to my mom and dad?"

"Know 'nuff to knowed that yer maw figured out I be yer paw's brother. It be ol' Ned that told 'dem that. Said that Edward Senior had a sea capt'n fer a brother. Said it be a Dussault feller. Well, yer maw, she found me and told me. Didn't believe her at first, but yer maw, she had a way to be convincin'."

Thinking back to his own personal memories of his mother, Edward smiled slightly and said "Yes she did Capt'n. Yes she did."

"Sadly, yer maw, she passed right after they git yer house all ready fer ya. 'Dis ol capt'n, he didn't git to spend a whole lotta time wit 'er, 'afore she did. But yer paw and me, we spent a whole lotta time together. Had lots o' lost time to make up, I'd expect."

"I'd expect Capt'n Petey. I couldn't even imagine what it would be like at this point in my life to discover that I had a brother I never knew about." Edward replied. "But one question Capt'n..."

"Yeah boy, what it be?" Captain Petey answered.

"How come my pop never told me about all this before he died? Figured he would have told me."

"Me boy, he tried. 'Member that one time ya was suppose to come over to the house fer a weekend 'bout a year after yer maw died?"

"Yeah. I had a breaking story to cover for the magazine and had to attend to it. Big story too about that mystery writer Harrison Weaver solving the years old murder of the girl from the Lost Colony outdoor play."

"Yeah, yer paw knowed that was important. That be why he didn't make no fuss 'bout it. But that be the time he was gonna tell you 'bout all of this. But you never come and then it was too late. Time went by, yer paw, he got sick, and he died too."

Feeling very guilty about all of this Edward replied, "That story wasn't bigger than anything my dad was going to tell me. I should have realized it before now. Now it's too late."

"Aye, boy, ain't this ol' capt'n's place to tell you what you shoulda done. But yer paw, he wanted you to know everything and told me everything. He knowed that you'd want to know. That why I went to da Ol' Country Kitchen lookin' fer ya after yer paw's services."

"That wasn't a coincidence that we ran into each other Capt'n?"

"No my laddie. I went there lookin' fer ya. I wanted to see if you was lookin' fir the answers 'bout the family."

“How did you know I did?” Edward asked.

“When I seen ya lookin’ at those pictures of yer paw dressed as ol’ Blackbeard at the diner, I kinda knowed you wanted to know more. That’s why I come up to ya and started jawin’ at you. But I wanted to make sure ya took the time to look fir answers yerself too. That be important to yer paw.”

“Thank you for being there for my dad, Captain Petey. I wished I was around more. And should have been.....”

Chapter 34

Back home in Bath, North Carolina now, Edward and Captain Petey spent some time going through the rest of his parent's things. They threw a lot of stuff out. They also kept a lot of things. Edward helped Captain Petey do some painting and cleaning, to make the house on King Street his own.

Edward had decided that the home will always be in the family, at least as long as Captain Petey was alive. It was to be the place that offered Captain Petey a place to stay warm and dry during storms. It was a place that Captain Petey was able to stay cool(ish) during the blazing heat of the summer. It was a place that Edward made many more frequent trips back to than he had in recent years. For some unknown reason, this house felt more like home than it had in a really long time. Edward found that feeling kind of strange since now it had an almost total stranger living in it, rather than his own parents.

But the stranger in the house on King Street was blood. He was the person that helped guide Edward toward the answers that he was searching for. About himself, his father, and his heritage.

The last thing Edward did that day, before leaving Bath for the Outer Banks, was to hang a sign on the mailbox that said "Home of Captain P. E. Thatcher Dussault."

Well, actually, the last thing Edward did before starting his trip, was to stop at the Old Country Kitchen for fried chicken and mashed potatoes. This time he stuck Capt'n Petey with the check.

Epilogue

Edward Drummond Thatcher Junior became as close to his uncle, Capt'n P. E. Thatcher Dussault as any man would become with his own father. And Capt'n Petey? Well, he treated Edward as the son he never had. Trips were made to both Bath and to the Outer Banks. One always making sure there was time for the other.

They lived this way for close to 25 years. Edward, turning his one magazine "empire" into a 5 magazine "empire." Employing enough people to allow Edward to not have to worry about all the day-to-day operations. Char had become the General Manager of all 5 publications. Billy stayed on to become the Editor-In-Chief. He even made it through a hurricane or two in the process.

Edward, eventually got married. She was a teller at Edward's bank and together they had a son that they named Edward Drummond Thatcher III. Or Trey as they called him. Trey grew up in the magazine business, went to the University of North Carolina at Chapel Hill, just like his dad before him. One day Edward would tell Trey the family history. He would tell him about Captain Edward Teach and Mary Ormond and the little boy she would call Lil' Neddie. Edward would tell Trey about the tunnel beneath the family home in Nags Head. He would explain Teach's Light. He would show him the family Bible that he still kept safe. It just wouldn't be today....

.

I said "I'd like to see you if you don't mind"
He said "I'd love to, dad, if I can find the time..."

Captain P. E. Thatcher Dussault lived in the house on King Street up to his last day. During those 25 years Capt'n Petey played the role of Blackbeard the Pirate at schools and county fairs around North Carolina. Picking up right where his brother had left off. When he wasn't playing the role of the pirate captain, Capt'n Petey could be found in one of two places: Sitting on the front porch of the house on King Street or at the Old Country Kitchen. Whether Captain Petey was here or there, he was doing the same thing. He was regaling, to whomever was in earshot, with stories of pirates and life on the sea as a fishing captain. 'Twas a good life Capt'n Petey often thought.

It was November 22nd, Thanksgiving Day that year, when Edward didn't get an answer to his knock on the door on King Street. Edward's wife and son had gone to Ohio to stay with her parents for the holiday. Edward wanted to spend it with his uncle. He knocked again. Still no answer. Edward pulled the keys out of his pocket and let himself in.

In the living room, in the high backed chair, Capt'n Petey's favorite, Edward found Capt'n Petey. He had passed sometime during the night. In his hands Capt'n Petey held "*Pyrates and Buccaneers of the Carolinas*." The book that started Edward on the path toward answering all of his questions.

A few days later, the town of Bath held another funeral at St Thomas Episcopal Church. The weather was unseasonably warm as they laid Peter Edward Thatcher Dussault into the grave next to his brother, underneath the giant oak.

The funeral was well attended and a get together was held after the burial at the Old Country Kitchen. Edward's wife and son had come from Ohio to be there. As was Katie and Hunter. Chief Haney came with his wife, as had Officer Meekins, his wife, Mary and their three younguns. Lined up on the walls of the diner were pics of both Edward Senior and his brother Petey dressed as Blackbeard the pirate.

That night, the heat and the humidity caused a late night thunderstorm in Bath. At around 2:30 in the morning a bright light appeared in the sky. It was a ball of fire larger than a man's head. It sailed back and forth from Plum Point to Archell Point over Bath Creek. Sitting on the front porch Edward watched the light moving back and forth, from one side to the other, without wavering its path from the wind. "Hello Captain Teach," Edward said softly. Having woke up from his sleep by the light, Trey joined his father on the porch. Looking at the strange light, Trey asked, "What in the blazes is that pop?"

With his foot, Edward pushed a chair over to his son and simply said, "Sit down boy. Have I got a story to tell you……"

Greg Smrdel has been many things in life, a father, radio DJ, hotel manager, trivia host, stand up comedian, writer, author and magazine editor. He continues to write about the things he loves the most, the Outer Banks of North Carolina.

You can contact Greg at www.gregsmrdel.com

Find his books at: www.amazon.com/author/gregsmrdel - or at select bookstores on the Outer Banks.

Like Greg on Facebook at Greg Smrdel, Ink for new releases, free giveaways and discounts on his books.

Made in the USA
Middletown, DE
19 October 2020

21638071R00104